Medieval Romance: The Falcon Queen

A Palace Tale of Betrayal, Power, and Survival — Court Intrigue Novels, Adult Historical Fiction

Chapter 1: A Princess Pledged, A Father's Whim 7

Chapter 2: Promises Made and Promises Broken 13

Chapter 3: A Title, A Palace, and A Rival 17

Chapter 4: A Hawk, A Friend, and a Secret 22

Chapter 5: A Lesson in Royal History 26

Chapter 6: The Queen in the Shadows 30

Chapter 7: A Season of Sickness and Sorrow 35

Chapter 8: The King's Fury 41

Chapter 9: An Ambassador's Warning 45

Chapter 10: The Hard Truth From a Friend 50

Chapter 11: A Farewell in Disguise 54

Chapter 12: The Usurper's Crown 57

Chapter 13: A Daughter's Birth, A Father's Rage 61

Chapter 14: Stripped of a Title, Made a Servant 66

Chapter 15: A Servant to the Princess 70

Chapter 16: The King's Oath, A Daughter's Defiance 73

Chapter 17: Whispers of a New Queen 76

Chapter 18: A Desperate Plan 80

Chapter 19: The King's Madness 84

Chapter 20: The Fall of the Falcon Queen 88

Chapter 21: The Price of Peace 93

Introduction

I remember the day like a wound that never quite healed: my father's voice pronouncing a pledge, the court's polite applause, and the sudden smallness of the chamber around me. At ten, fury rose like a tide — hot, immediate, and undeniable. That fury was not merely childish temper; it became my first weapon and later my most guarded truth. The story that follows begins with that single, bitter promise and traces how a life ordered by others learns to answer on its own terms. For many readers, the challenge of palace stories is the distance between golden ritual and human longing. Courts glitter, but behind the banners are choices that cost dearly; the everyday cruelties and comforts shape destinies as surely as any battle. The central struggle here is not just between houses or nations, but between roles imposed and identities discovered. The protagonist faces the common problem of those born into obligation: how to keep a self that others expect to belong to them. This novel offers a particular answer: through small resistances, unexpected alliances, and the slow education of courage. Rather than a single grand rebellion, the heroine's transformation arrives through choices, betrayals, and loyalties tested. The book traces political maneuvering and intimate tenderness alike, presenting a pathway from reluctant pawn to a woman who carves power from peril. You will find the tale arranged as a sequence of seasons: the betrothal and its immediate fallout; rising intrigues and shifting loyalties; a desperate counterplan and its costs; and the aftermath, where peace demands a price. Each section reveals a layer of court life and the private decisions that change history.

Chapter 1: A Princess Pledged, A Father's Whim

I have King Henry's fiery temper. No one would deny that. The day I learned he had betrothed me to the French king, I exploded.

"I cannot believe my father would pledge me to that disgusting old man!" I raged. I hurled the bed pillows onto my chamber floor. "I shall not, not, NOT marry him!"

I was only ten years old. I had not yet mastered my anger or learned to use it as a weapon. I shouted and stamped my feet. At last, my fury gave way to gusts of tears. Between sobs, I glanced at my governess, the long-nosed Lady Margaret. She was the countess of Salisbury. She continued stitching her needlework as if nothing was happening.

"Come now," the countess soothed, her needle flicking in and out. "It is only a betrothal. That is a long way from marriage, as you know. Besides, madam, the king wishes it."

Her calm made me even angrier. "I don't care what he wishes! My father pays so little attention to me. I doubt he even remembers who I am!"

A thin smile creased Salisbury's face. She set down her embroidery hoop. She dabbed my cheeks with a fine linen handkerchief. "He knows, dear Mary, he knows. You grow more like him every day. You have his fair skin, his lively blue eyes, his shining red-gold hair." She tucked the handkerchief into her sleeve and sighed. "And, unfortunately, his temper as well."

Suddenly exhausted, I threw myself onto my great bed. "When is it to be, Salisbury?" I murmured.

"King Francis and his court will arrive in April for the Feast of Saint George. We have three months to prepare. The royal dressmaker will soon start on your new gown." She continued, "Your mother, the queen, sent word that she favors green trimmed with white. You are also to have a cloak made of cloth of gold."

"I hate green," I grumbled. This was a battle I might win. My gentle, patient mother could be as stubborn as my father. "And I do not care if green and white are our royal colors!"

"It seems that madam dislikes nearly everything today," Salisbury said. "Perhaps the world will look better in the morning."

"It will not."

"Nevertheless, madam, it is time for prayers."

I slid down from my high mattress. I knelt on the cold stone floor beside my governess. We did this every night and every morning. Together we recited our prayers. When we finished, two serving maids came to remove my kirtle (an outer dress) and dress me in my silk sleeping shirt. They snuffed out the candles until only one remained. I climbed back onto my high bedstead. Propped on one elbow, I watched my governess stretch out on the narrow trundle bed beside mine. She drew up the satin coverlet. Salisbury was tall, and the coverlet was short. When she pulled it to her sharp chin, her feet stuck out. It was the first time all day I had felt like laughing.

Soon after my eleventh birthday in spring 1527, I teetered on a stool. I was Mary Tudor, daughter of King Henry VIII and Queen Catherine of Aragon. The royal dressmaker and her assistants pushed and pulled at my betrothal gown. They pinned and tucked the heavy green silk. Would they ever be finished? My head ached, and my stomach felt queasy.

"Come, madam," the dressmaker coaxed. "You want to please your bridegroom, do you not?"

"No, I do not," I snapped. I had overheard everything from the gossiping ladies of the household. Francis, king of France, was ugly and repulsive. He was a lecherous old man with warts, pockmarks, and foul breath.

"But your father, the king, wishes it," the dressmaker reminded me.

I sighed and stood straight and motionless. *Your father, the king, wishes it.* How I dreaded those words! The French king and his court would soon arrive. I would obey my father's wishes. I would place my small hand in the grisly paw of the horrible Francis. I would promise to be his bride.

Finally, the gown was ready and the preparations were complete. My trunks were packed for the journey to London from my palace in Ludlow. Traveling with my group of courtiers and ladies-in-waiting, Salisbury and I were carried in the royal litter. It was lined with padded silk and velvet cushions. Two white horses bore it between them. After nearly two weeks of bumping over washed-out roads, we arrived. We were muddy and bedraggled at Greenwich Palace on the River Thames.

I ran through the palace to find my mother. I found myself surrounded by commotion. New tapestries hung on the walls of the Great Hall. The royal musicians and costumers arranged masques and other entertainments. Carts delivered provisions for the banquets to the palace kitchens.

Despite the excitement, I felt unwell. As the arrival of the French king neared, I suffered from headaches. I also had a queasy stomach. My physician treated me with doses of foul-tasting potions, but they did no good.

Then word came that storms had delayed the ships carrying King Francis. My bridegroom would not arrive until the weather cleared. An idea came to me. Maybe his ship will be lost. Maybe he will drown and I will never have to marry him. The thought had barely crossed my mind before I regretted it. I would have to admit these wicked thoughts to my confessor. Then I would do penance and receive absolution, as I had been taught.

But since I had already committed such a sin, I decided to turn it to my advantage. I knelt on the hard stone floor with my spine straight as a lance. My hands were clasped beneath my chin, my eyes turned toward Heaven. I prayed, *Dear God, if it is thy will to take King Francis, please send a good husband in his place!* I was not sure what a good husband was. For that, I put my trust in God.

For nearly three weeks the storms raged. Then they suddenly weakened. Toward mid-April, King Francis and his huge retinue landed in Dover. They made their way to Greenwich, escorted by my father's knights.

"Perhaps he won't find me to his satisfaction after all," I said hopefully to Salisbury.

"That is improbable, madam," said Salisbury. Her plain face was as serene as ever. "The French king requested a portrait, which your father sent him. It was presented in an ivory box with the Tudor rose carved on the cover. King Francis much liked the sweet face he saw in it."

How infuriating! "Salisbury, why must it be this way? If I had asked for his portrait to see if he pleased me, would I have gotten it?"

Salisbury laughed. "Unlikely. That is not how the world works."

"Well, it should be," I grumbled, although I knew she was right.

The festival honoring Saint George began with an evening banquet. This would be my first glimpse of the man I would be betrothed to. As King Francis entered the Great Hall, I could see he was nearly as tall as my father. But he was much thinner, except for a small, round belly. He was seated at one end of the king's table, and I was at the other. I have always been shortsighted. At a distance, I could not see his features clearly. All I could see were his white hands fluttering about like startled pigeons. But I could hear his laugh, which sounded like a braying donkey.

As I peered toward him, trumpeters announced the first course. It included two dozen dishes of frumenty with venison, salted hart, and roast swan. There were also lamprey, pike, heron, carp, kid, and mutton pasties. The second course followed with just as many dishes. These included crayfish, prawns, oysters, conger eel, and baked larks.

The custom was to have only a small taste of each dish. It was a hard custom to observe, especially with prawns and oysters. I was very fond of these delicacies. But when I saw the white hands flying about at the other end of the table, I lost my appetite. Imagine having to live with this for the rest of my life! I found I could scarcely swallow.

The banquet concluded with a grand dessert. It was a replica of Noah's ark, nearly three feet tall and made entirely of sugar. A procession of every kind of animal, molded of almond paste, paraded up the boat's gangplank. On the deck stood a miniature couple, Noah and his wife. Then my father pointed at the figures and called out loudly, "Look! The king of France and our own dear Princess of Wales!"

The company sent up a cheer. As expected, I lowered my eyes and smiled. But I wanted nothing more than to run from the table. When the feasting ended, it was time to present King Francis and his courtiers to my mother and me. This was the moment I had dreaded. The courtiers came first, speaking to me in French, Latin, and Italian. They asked me my age in three different languages. I replied easily, but my attention was on King Francis, who moved ever closer. I could now clearly see his watery eyes and long, beak-like nose. The French king then bent over my hand and kissed it wetly. I nearly gagged. "The jewel of England," my father told Francis proudly. "My pearl of the world." How could my father do this to me?

After the banquet, Henry entertained his French guests with a bearbaiting. I sat beside my father as an enormous blind bear called Jack was led into the bear ring. The king's bearward (a bear's keeper) let loose a pack of dogs. Jack struck out sightlessly. With one swipe of his paw, he killed the first two mastiffs that rushed at his throat. Several more dogs were released into the ring. Soon, the bear and dogs were bloody and dazed. Jack staggered around the ring, his fur matted with blood. The noise was deafening, the stench of blood sickening. The bearward looked up at my father for a signal.

"What shall it be, my darling princess?" my father asked. "Is it life or death for poor old Jack? You must say!"

I was quite dazed from the gory sight. "I say let him be killed!" I declared in a trembling voice. I knew that was what my father wanted me to say. But I wished with all my heart that I had the power to save the bear's life.

"Well said!" my father shouted. He made a sign to the bearward. The bearward sent in one last dog to lunge at the wounded bear's throat. I watched the huge animal fall and die. I glanced at my betrothed, King Francis. His hands still fluttered, although he looked a bit pale. At least his donkey-like bray was silenced.

Three days after the banquet, I stood stiffly between King Henry and Queen Catherine. I was dressed in the new green-and-white silk gown for the betrothal ceremony. The golden robe trailing from my shoulders was so long and heavy I needed six attendants. So many sparkling necklaces were draped around my neck that I thought I would choke. Francis leered at me. He slipped a diamond and ruby ring on my finger.

How much more of this must I endure? I wondered. Again I felt cramping and nausea. Tears might have gathered, but I had been trained not to weep in public. "Ista puella nunquam plorat," my father used to boast in Latin. "This girl never cries." He did not know how much I cried when I was alone.

That evening there was another lavish banquet. When the meal ended, the king signaled me to leave the table and prepare for the masque. This was another of my father's ideas. He loved dressing up in elaborate outfits. He had ordered me and fifteen others to be costumed in attire suggesting the Far North. I liked the fur-trimmed costumes, and I truly enjoyed dancing.

Since arriving at Greenwich, my dancing tutor had rehearsed us until we knew the dance perfectly.

During these rehearsals, I had noticed a particular lady-in-waiting in my mother's court. The lady's thick black hair, gleaming like a raven's wing, was left to fly wild. Other women tucked theirs modestly beneath a hood. Her eyes were shiny and black as onyx. Her skin was pale as milk, and her body was thin and supple. A black ribbon circled her neck with a large diamond at her throat. She stood out among the rosy-skinned ladies with their pale blue eyes. My mother's forty-nine ladies-in-waiting wore pretty, bright gowns, but this one dressed in dramatic black and white. The lady's name was Anne Boleyn. By eavesdropping, I had learned she was the daughter of England's ambassador to the French court. She had grown up in France. Soon after she and her sister returned, my mother had invited them to join her court. Anne spoke French in a playful, mocking manner. It was quite different from the formal French of my tutors. She was witty, clever, and her frequent laughter attracted everyone. She was not of royal blood—she was called simply Lady Anne. Yet she behaved as though she were. I thought her fascinating.

The masque began. I led the seven ladies, including Anne, out of a make-believe ice cave. There we were joined by eight men swirling long fur capes. The velvet half mask hiding King Henry's eyes did not hide his identity. He was always the tallest man in any crowd. When we paired off as planned, the masked king held out his hand to me. We danced the stately pavane. But as we performed the complicated steps, I noticed something. My father's eyes were not on me but followed the black-haired dancer. There was an eagerness in his look that I had never seen before. It troubled me. I needed to learn more about this Anne Boleyn.

Chapter 2: Promises Made and Promises Broken

"You have nothing to worry about for now," Salisbury assured me. We were starting our journey back to Ludlow on a glowing May morning. Dew sparkled on the hedges. The air smelled sweet with blossoms. "Before he sailed for France, King Francis complained to your father. He said, 'The princess is so small and frail that no marriage is possible for three years.'"

"'Small and frail'—is that what he said?" I cried. "So I do not please him after all! Why did he not say this before we were betrothed?"

"You please him well, madam. He simply worries that you may not be strong enough to bear children. But this should not concern you." Salisbury added, "My prayers are answered. You will have plenty of time to grow. And who knows what may happen?"

"I shall never marry!" I moaned. "I hate the men my father chooses for me! If I do not satisfy a pompous old man like Francis, then who can I satisfy?"

This was my third betrothal. The first had been to the dauphin, the eldest son of this same King Francis. It took place when I was barely two years old. We still lived with both my parents at Greenwich Palace. I could remember almost nothing of that event. But Salisbury had often described the occasion for me.

All I could recall was a jowly man in scarlet satin looming over me. It was Cardinal Wolsey, my father's bloated friend. He placed a ring with a large sparkling stone on my finger. Wolsey, with his long yellow teeth and cold gray eyes, had always frightened me. I also remember looking up at my father and smiling at him. My father smiled back. How I adored him! I loved being carried proudly on his shoulder around the Great Hall. He would show me off or feed me dainty bits from his own plate. My mother would frown in disapproval. Then, four years later when I was nearly six, my father changed his mind. Marrying me to the dauphin was not in England's best interests. The betrothal was broken.

My mother and Salisbury explained the situation. From the time of my birth, my father had considered choices for my husband. I was my parents' only living child. These were not even husbands, but promises of a husband. Many promises could be made and broken before a real wedding.

"A daughter is not as prized as a son," Salisbury said. "But a princess is still precious. She is a valuable tool for forging alliances between kingdoms. You must not concern yourself with it, Mary. You have no say in any of it." She continued, "Your mother, the queen, had no say when her own father betrothed her to Prince Henry. These are the affairs of men, and especially of kings."

I loudly protested this idea. My father adored me! Surely my happiness was most important to him.

"Your happiness has nothing to do with it, madam," Salisbury said in her infuriatingly calm way. To my sorrow, I learned that Salisbury was right. My happiness never mattered.

After the dauphin, King Henry next chose my Spanish cousin, Charles. He was the son of my mother's sister. I was just six, and Charles was a man of twenty-two. He held the title of Holy Roman Emperor.

When I was betrothed to Charles, a magnificent procession traveled from London to Dover. My mother and I rode in our royal litter. Crowds of people lined the route, cheering and tossing their caps. At Dover, we met Charles. Charles had sailed from Spain with 180 ships. He arrived in Dover with two thousand courtiers and servants. When I finally saw him, his appearance surprised me. He was dressed in a peculiar way, so different from my father's crimson velvet. Charles wore black velvet with only a gold chain around his neck. He had kind, intelligent eyes. He also praised me when I played a little song for him on my virginals (a small harpsichord). I liked him, although he was sixteen years older than me.

King Henry owned many palaces and manor houses. He had prepared Bridewell, one of the most beautiful, for the emperor's visit. During his stay of several months, Charles began to teach me to play chess.

Then the visit was over. The day before he sailed away, Charles kissed my hand. He promised to return to claim me as his wife when I reached the marriageable age of twelve. But one day, more than a year after his departure, a page came with a message. I broke the wax seal and read it. The king wished to see me at once. He had signed it, as always, *Henricus Rex*—Henry the King.

I immediately picked up my skirts and ran happily to the king's chambers. I ran down the long gallery and up the king's staircase. I went through several chambers crowded with guards, officials, and advisors. Finally, I entered the privy chamber. The king was seated at a great oak table with Cardinal Wolsey at his side. Breathless, I fell to my knees before my father. I bowed my head for his blessing.

I seldom saw my father, who was usually performing his kingly duties. When I did see him, the visits were usually merry. But this time the purpose was entirely serious.

"You must write to Charles immediately," the king said.

A quill, inkhorn, and parchment were fetched. I climbed onto a seat at the table. Cardinal Wolsey himself sharpened the quill for me. I waited for my father's instructions.

"You shall write in Latin, of course," the king ordered. This was not a problem. Even at age eight, I could write in both Latin and English. "Speak of your deep fondness for the emperor. Hint at your jealousy that he has sought the affections of another. Then swear your devotion. Can you do that, Mary?"

"Yes, my lord," I replied. I had no idea what he was talking about. Jealousy? Affections of another? But I dared not ask. I dipped the quill and began to write while my father paced, dictating the words. The king slipped a ring from his own finger to send with the letter. The ring was set with a large, brilliant green stone. "The emerald reflects the truth of lovers," the king explained, though it was no explanation to me. "It will change color if one of the lovers is unfaithful."

Unfaithful?

He then turned to Wolsey, seemingly forgetting I was there. I backed slowly out of my father's chamber. Salisbury had taught me never to turn my back on the king. I hurried to find Salisbury to ask for an explanation. My governess reached for a silver comb and began pulling it through my curls. "The rumor has reached the king," she said quietly. "Charles is thinking of marrying someone else."

"But Charles is betrothed to me!" I pouted, pulling away from the comb.

"Your father must be certain of Charles's loyalty," she said.

Weeks later, my father burst unannounced into my mother's chambers. His face was dark with anger. His eyes shot sparks of fury. The waiting ladies scattered like frightened doves. I dropped to my knees, hoping he would not notice me. My mother serenely laid aside her needlework and rose to greet him.

"Damn the Spaniard!" he roared. "The emerald has changed color! Charles has broken his pledge and married a Portuguese princess!" He turned and stalked out, slamming the door.

"Will my father find me another husband?" I asked when I dared to speak.

"Of course he will, Mary," my mother assured me. "Never fear."

I resumed my stitching. I was disappointed, for I truly liked Charles. I was too young to be grateful that, for the moment, I was as free as I would ever be. For a time, I heard no more talk of future husbands. Instead, I received another message from the king. I was to be crowned Princess of Wales. I was nine years old.

Chapter 3: A Title, A Palace, and A Rival

My crowning ceremony caused a giddy uproar. I was to have a new gown of pale blue silk. It was embroidered with tiny flowers and trimmed in gold. Even Queen Catherine, who cared little for fine clothes, ordered a new gown. I had not seen my mother so happy in a long time.

"This means your father has decided you will one day be queen," my mother said. She kissed my forehead. "So the illegitimate Fitzroy is not in line for the throne, thank God."

I had heard a little about this "illegitimate Fitzroy." He was the king's natural son, named Henry Fitzroy. *Fitzroy* means "son of the king." While Henry was the father, the child's mother was not my mother, his wife. The mother was a woman named Bessie Blount. It interested me that I had a baby brother hidden away somewhere. I knew I must not speak of him, especially to my mother. Someday I would ask Salisbury about this illegitimate half-brother. For now, I was happy to be the center of attention.

On the day of the ceremony, King Henry entered with a flourish of horns. He was accompanied by many earls, barons, and their servants. Cardinal Wolsey was there, of course, dressed all in scarlet. He showed his terrible teeth in something like a smile. But the smile never reached his glittering eyes.

I shivered and turned to my father. How magnificent he looked! He wore close-fitting hose that showed off his muscular legs. Over these, he wore red velvet trunk hose stuffed to an onion shape. They were slashed to show hints of silver underneath. His jacket of quilted black velvet was covered in pearls and jewels. In my eyes, King Henry was the handsomest man in the world.

"Are you ready, my princess?" the king asked.

"I am, Your Majesty," I said, dropping into a deep curtsy.

The musty chapel was lit by hundreds of flickering candles. The ceremony droned on tediously. My beautiful gown was hot and uncomfortable. Still, I moved smoothly through my part, as Salisbury had trained me. I knelt before my father as he set a jeweled coronet on my head. He invested me with my new title, Princess of Wales. I gazed up at him, basking in his approval. "My perfect pearl of the world," he called me. "The jewel of all England."

Several days after the royal banquet in my honor, I learned my father was sending me far away. He did not tell me himself. Wolsey brought me the news. The cardinal sat on a stool in my schoolroom. His fat fingers were spread over his fat thighs. He had brought me a beautifully illustrated book of hours as a gift. Then he added, almost as an afterthought, "Princess Mary, the king has given orders. You are to move to Ludlow Palace, near the Welsh border. You will establish your own court." He continued, "The queen will not accompany you. Lady Margaret, countess of Salisbury, will go with you instead. You are to leave in two weeks, madam."

I felt my lips begin to tremble. I was determined not to let him see how upset I was. I stared hard at his heavy gold cardinal's ring. "My mother is not to accompany me? But why?"

"Because the king wishes it," rumbled the cardinal. He heaved his large body off the stool. He held out his ring. Hiding my disgust, I bent to kiss it.

It was not that I had never been away from my mother. We were often separated. She would be at one palace with my father, and I at another with nurses and tutors. But she was never more than a few hours away. We saw one another often. Ludlow was a journey of ten days, even in good weather. I would see her only rarely. Later, when the cardinal had gone, I wept on my mother's knee. But I received little comfort.

"No good will come of your tears," the queen warned. "Your father, the king, wishes it. And so it shall be. But remember you are now one step closer to the throne. This is the beginning of your training to rule as queen." She went on, "Salisbury is my dearest friend. She will act as your mother in my place. And we shall write to one another as often as we wish. When your father summons us to his court, we shall all be together."

My household would number three hundred. This included the privy council that would govern in my name. It also included a staff of servants. Days were spent packing belongings into wooden carts. I was used to moving. When my father held court, we stayed in the great palaces near London. Each summer he went on progress, journeying into the countryside for his subjects to see him. In autumn he hunted. Often my mother and I went with him. But this journey was different. My heart was so heavy that I slept little and ate nothing for days.

The night before our departure, my father summoned me to his chambers. He gave me his blessing. I was angry and upset, but I could not show it. I wanted to cry out, "Why?" but I was silent. My mother was present, and I ached to throw myself into her arms. I sensed my father would not like such a display. I had to behave like a future queen. My mother's kiss that night seemed cool and dry.

On a late summer day, I sat miserably with Salisbury in my royal litter. The procession would stretch for miles, protected by royal guards. As the trumpets sounded, I looked up for a last glimpse of my mother. She stood at her open window, waving. I watched her handkerchief flutter as we clattered out of the gates.

"When can we return?" I asked Salisbury frantically.

"Christmastime," she answered calmly. Christmastime was nearly four months away. It seemed an unbearably long time. As our procession moved toward Ludlow, villagers turned out to wave and cheer. "Greet your people, madam," Salisbury instructed. "They're saluting you."

"I do not feel like it," I protested.

"Feel like it or not, you are a princess," Salisbury reminded me. "Smile and wave." Obediently, I smiled and raised my royal hand.

I missed my mother terribly. Receiving a letter from her brightened my days. I would rush to my room to compose a reply. My attempts to write cheerful letters were always defeated by my longing for her. I complained often. The queen wrote regularly to Salisbury with instructions for my care. She insisted upon discipline and simple food. I spent too much time protesting the boiled meat and plain bread. I would later regret wasting time on such unimportant matters.

I also complained about my tutor. King Henry, a man of sharp intellect, had ordered that my studies must be rigorous. He hired a noted Spanish scholar, Juan Luis Vives, to oversee them. Master Vives was thin-lipped and ill-tempered. Tufts of dark hair sprouted from his ears. He always carried a walking stick with a silver fox's head on top. I thought it resembled the tutor himself. "I see you have been badly spoiled," the tutor purred. Then he roared like a lion: "I believe children should feel the rod upon their backs at least once a day."

Terrified, I bent over my lesson book. Master Vives paced back and forth, smacking the stick into his palm. It whirred as he slashed it through the air. Every time I made an error, I was sure he would strike me. At the end of my long hours with Vives, I would run to hide my face in Salisbury's lap.

"Don't be afraid of him," Salisbury comforted me. "Your mother has made it plain that he is not to lay a hand upon you."

"But what about that awful stick?"

"No, he may not strike you with that." But what if he forgot my mother's orders? I was never comforted for long.

I loathed my tutor almost as much as I loved my governess. Salisbury taught me manners and court behavior. I learned all the rules for sitting, standing, kneeling, eating, and every other public act. The lessons were excruciatingly boring, but Salisbury was always patient. She also taught me the larger lessons for a future queen. I learned to be gracious even when I felt ill, tired, or sad. I had to show mercy even to those I believed did not deserve it. I had to control my anger. This was the most difficult lesson of all.

At last, the Christmas season arrived. As Salisbury had promised, there was an invitation to court. I loved court life—the pretty gowns, the jewels, and the banquets. The long journey from Ludlow to Greenwich Palace seemed not so long. There would be time with my mother and perhaps a visit with my father. There would be music and dancing every night. My father would show me off, the Princess of Wales. I would be the center of attention.

But when the season ended, I had to return to Ludlow. Although my heart ached to say farewell to my mother, I did not weep. "Until Easter, then," I said, assuming I would be called to court again.

"Perhaps," she said. "We can at least hope."

I counted the weeks until Easter, but no invitation arrived. The next great court festival was Whitsuntide, at the end of May. Again I waited, nearly ill with impatience. I was not allowed to write to my father and beg for an invitation. But I sent my mother many letters, pleading with her to send for me. Her replies were warm, but she did not answer my questions. Why was I not called to court? When will I see you again?

Instead, I received a summons from the king to come to Bridewell for another ceremony. This time, my half-brother, Henry Fitzroy, would be the focus. At this ceremony, King Henry intended to give Fitzroy a string of royal titles. He would become Duke of Somerset, Duke of Richmond, and more. It would have done no good to complain. And I was thrilled at the chance to be with my mother. But when we reached Bridewell, I found Queen Catherine in no mood for chatter. She was furious.

"Fitzroy will receive all these titles and have a household even greater than yours, Mary," she fumed. She turned to Salisbury. "Imagine a six-year-old illegitimate child outranking a princess!" she hissed. Then she whispered angrily to me, "Clearly you are no longer the king's choice to inherit the throne. He intends to put his illegitimate son in your rightful place. The people will not stand for it, nor will I."

Throughout the long ceremony, I observed my rival. He was a pretty boy with golden curls, wrapped in ermine and jewels. He looked thoroughly miserable, and I felt a little sorry for him. But only a little. After the last trumpet fanfares, my mother swept off to protest to the king. I waited fearfully outside the privy chamber. My father stormed out, rushing past me without seeing me. His face was blood-red and his eyes were small points of rage. When he was gone, I tiptoed to my mother's side.

"It is no use," the queen said, slumped wearily in her chair. "He will not listen. And now to punish me, he is taking away my three most cherished ladies-in-waiting. He is sending them back to Spain. I shall be so alone!" That was the first time I had known my father to rebuke my mother. It frightened me deeply. I did not know it then, but Anne Boleyn's poison had already begun its deadly work. Nor did I know I would not see my parents for nearly a year. By the time of my betrothal to King Francis, Anne's poison was eating at my father's soul.

Chapter 4: A Hawk, A Friend, and a Secret

After my betrothal to Francis, I was relieved to return to Ludlow. But soon there was another change of home. My father did not write; Wolsey sent the message. I was to move to Richmond Palace. I did not understand why, but I was glad. Richmond was beautiful, with a great tower and slim turrets. It was close to London, only a few hours' journey by barge from Greenwich.

I settled in quickly at Richmond. One summer evening, I set out to explore the grounds with my favorite attendant, Lady Susan. Only with Susan did I feel a true friendship. Susan had flame-red hair and was clever and adventurous. She was the daughter of the Duke of Norfolk, one of my father's closest advisers. But there was something more: Susan was Anne Boleyn's cousin. I had often thought of how my father looked at Lady Anne as we danced. Their image sent a shiver of danger through me. And though I felt drawn to Susan, I knew not to ask about her dramatic cousin—at least not yet.

As Susan and I walked, we came upon a tall, thin boy. He carried a small living thing in his cupped hands. I told him to show me what he had. He carefully opened his hands to reveal a newly hatched hawk, quaking with fright.

"Who are you?" I asked the boy.

"Peter Cheseman," he said. "My father is assistant to the royal falconer."

"And that bird?" I asked. "Does it have a name?"

"No, madam. This one is no good," he explained. "See, she is injured. My father says it is worthless to try to train her. But I mean to prove him wrong."

"And so you shall," I told him boldly. I had no idea how a lowborn boy like Peter had a better chance than I, a princess, of proving a father wrong.

Lady Susan took a special interest in the injured bird. After that, she and I found excuses to visit it often. One day we found Peter in distress.

"A cat got her," he blurted out. "It was my fault."

"It was not your fault, Peter!" Lady Susan insisted. "I'm sure you did all you could. If not for the cat, she would have been a fine hunter!" Peter looked at Susan gratefully. I wished I had been the one to offer him such reassurance.

Toward the end of summer, the hawks finished their molt. New feathers replaced the old ones, and they became active hunters again. Nearly every day after my lessons, I went with Lady Susan to the mews (a place where hawks are kept). We watched as Peter and his father trained different types of falcons. One afternoon we found Peter in the weathering yard. He was coaxing a young hawk to fly from its perch to his fist. Finally, the bird spread its wings and glided to Peter's gloved fist. Peter rewarded it with a small piece of meat.

"Soon this one will be ready to fly in the open," he said, smiling. "And then she'll be ready to hunt."

Peter explained the bird's lessons. First, it must learn to sit by its captured prey but not eat it. Once that is mastered, it must fly with its kill to the falconer's fist. "No one needs to teach her to hunt—that she's born knowing," he said. "Teaching her to trust you is the hard part. It's no good if she goes off with her prey and sits in a tree."

I left the yard and hurried to Salisbury. "I wish to study the art of falconry," I announced. I argued that my father hunted with falcons. My mother also used to ride out with the king, a small falcon on her gloved fist. Salisbury wrote to Queen Catherine. She sent her approval with a gift of silver bells for the bird's leg and a soft leather hood. When the gifts arrived, I rushed to the mews to show them to Peter.

"Now," he said, "we must find you a hawk, and you'll learn together."

Peter trapped a young hawk, a merlin with eyes the color of marigolds. This was to be my bird. "It's the females that are wanted," he told me. "They're bigger and stronger than the males." I named the merlin Noisette, the French word for "hazelnut," because of her lovely color.

"We have to get her used to her new life among people," Peter said. "And there must always be a reward for her. If you don't reward her, she won't work for you. You can't force her. She will fly away and never come back." He continued, "But you must not reward her too much. When she is full, she will not hunt. She'll do best when she's a bit lean. That's when you take her out. If you've trained her right, she'll come back when you whistle."

It took me days to learn the whistle that would bring Noisette to my glove. Once I mistakenly practiced it during my Latin grammar lesson. Master Vives bashed his walking stick so hard on my desk that the silver fox head was bent afterward.

Finally, Noisette and I were ready. Mounted on my white pony, I squinted up at the brilliant sky. On my left hand, I wore a thick leather glove. High overhead, Noisette circled lazily. Several of my ladies had ridden out with me. All but Lady Susan straggled behind, gossiping. Susan and I trotted on ahead. Beside us rode the pompous royal falconer, Lord Ellington. I leaned back, searching for Peter. He saw me and grinned. I had become fond of Peter during the weeks of training. Unlike my weak eyes, Peter's seemed as keen as the hawks he worked with. I admired his way with birds. He was patient and firm, unlike Master Vives.

I sometimes wondered if it might be possible to marry him. He would surely make a fine companion. He would let me rule England, just as he let me do whatever I wanted. But I knew that was impossible. I could no more choose my own husband than fly like Noisette. Noisette circled slowly overhead. I gazed up at her, thrilled. For a moment, I imagined I was that merlin, flying free and solitary. I was never alone. Salisbury slept beside my bed, and two servant girls lay near the door. From morning until my nightly prayers, I was always surrounded by people.

Suddenly Noisette spotted her prey. She tucked in her wings and dived, snatching a lark out of the air. I envied her freedom, her solitude, and her deadly power. I whistled, and Noisette came to my fist with the lark in her talons. The falconer took the lark. I presented Noisette with her reward, a bit of meat. Riding home at the end of the day, I wondered if my father knew I was learning one of his favorite sports. I thought of him far more often than he seemed to think of me. My mother wrote nearly every week, but it had been months since I had a word from the king.

"Why does he not come to visit me?" I asked Susan days later. The weather had turned foul. "Deer hunting is one of his favorite pastimes. Why then do I hear nothing from him?"

"They say the king has taken up falconry again," Susan replied mysteriously.

"Then he could come and hunt with me! He could bring my mother as well. Why does he not bring the queen here, so I may see them both?"

"His hunting companion is not the queen," Susan said in a low voice. "It is my cousin, Anne Boleyn."

Her words took my breath away. "Lady Anne? But why?"

"It is said the king is in love with Anne," Susan replied, looking down.

"What lies are you telling me?" I demanded furiously.

"Sadly, madam, it is the truth. The king makes no secret of his passion. My father speaks of it proudly. King Henry is seen everywhere with Lady Anne. Queen Catherine appears with him only at large public occasions."

"I don't believe you!" I cried. I turned and splashed back to my chambers through the rain.

As a servant girl helped me with my wet clothes, I saw a letter on my table. It bore Cardinal Wolsey's seal. His letters seldom brought good news. I waited until I was dry to break the seal. It was a message from the king, commanding me to come to Greenwich for Christmas. At last, I had been invited. My mood lifted at once. But then a darker thought crossed my mind: Anne Boleyn would surely be there. I remembered how my father had looked at Anne. And now Susan claimed my father was in love with her. I vowed not to believe these hurtful rumors until I saw proof with my own eyes. I would have that chance at Christmas.

Chapter 5: A Lesson in Royal History

For the next month, my lessons seemed longer and duller than ever. My eyes burned, my head throbbed, and my body ached with fatigue. All I could think about was what I would find when I traveled to Greenwich for Christmas. I was studying *Utopia*, a book by my father's friend Sir Thomas More. I found the work difficult. I was forbidden to read books of chivalry and romance for entertainment. Meanwhile, my ladies-in-waiting played cards and rolled dice to amuse themselves. I longed to join them, but I was not allowed such simple pastimes.

The hours crawled by. All day, tutors in various subjects took their turns. In some classes, a few court ladies participated, but usually I studied alone. My eyelids would droop, and Master Vives would shriek in my ear. "Pay attention! Do not try to avoid the task!" Only after the formal lessons were over did Salisbury, my beloved governess, teach me what I truly needed to know.

One November night, a storm rattled the windows of my bedchamber. My governess began a long story. "Mary, you know some of this story," she began. "But perhaps you have not understood what it means. You must understand it now. I believe that grave changes lie ahead. You must be prepared." I lay perfectly still under the thick satin coverlet. "Go on, I beg you."

"Under your grandfather's rule, England prospered," she said. "The royal treasury was full. He intended for his older son, Arthur, to succeed him. While still a young man, Arthur was betrothed. The wife your grandfather chose for him was Catherine of Aragon, daughter of Spain's rulers."

"My mother."

"Yes, sweet Mary, but this was long before you were born. Catherine was sixteen when she married Arthur. I was a guest at the wedding. I can still picture Princess Catherine riding a fine Spanish mule to the church. That was the custom of her people." She continued, "It was at her wedding that she met your father. Prince Henry was just a cheerful, pink-cheeked boy, barely ten years old. It was November, in the year 1501. The sky was covered with heavy, gray clouds. Henry's cheerful smile must have warmed Catherine's heart. But soon her heart was chilled. Only a few months later, Arthur died of consumption."

I sighed, thinking of my mother's sorrow.

"The king did not want to send Catherine and her dowry back to Spain. The two kings, Henry and Ferdinand, devised a solution. Catherine would be kept in England to marry Arthur's younger brother, Henry. He had not yet reached his eleventh birthday." Salisbury explained, "Many theologians believed such marriages were forbidden by Scripture. But the pope in Rome granted a special permission. This allowed Henry to marry his brother's widow. Henry and Catherine were then betrothed."

"But my father was too young to wed, was he not?" I asked.

"He was then," Salisbury agreed. "Six years passed. Catherine spent those years living a quiet, pious life. It was during this time that your mother and I became close friends."

"And my father?" I asked. "Did you know him as well?"

"I knew him as all of England did. We watched as the lively boy grew into a man. He grew very tall, with merry blue eyes and red-gold hair. He was strong as a bear and graceful as a deer. Your father was a magnificent man! When his own father died, the young prince inherited great wealth and the crown. Shortly after, Henry and Catherine were wed."

"The young couple spent their last honeymoon night at the Tower of London. The next morning they rode in a golden litter to Westminster Abbey. There, Henry and Catherine were crowned rulers of England. I was by your mother's side, happy for her."

"How old was my mother then?" I asked. The hour was late, but I was wide awake.

"She was twenty-three, and your father was seventeen. The celebration went on for days. You would have loved it, Mary! 'Long live King Henry the Eighth!' we cried. 'Long live Queen Catherine!'"

Outside, the storm howled. I marveled that my governess was telling me this now. Why was she telling me this story? Soon dawn would arrive, and I would face another day of Master Vives. But I wanted to know everything. "And you were with my mother then?" I prompted.

"Yes, I came to your mother's court as a lady-in-waiting. I saw how deeply Henry fell in love with his bride. That she was older seemed only to deepen his passion. Their first child, a girl, was stillborn." She continued, "But when Queen Catherine delivered a living son, the king seemed more in love than ever. How King Henry celebrated! Cannons boomed, shattering windows. Public fountains flowed with wine. The feasting and dancing went on for days. King Henry arranged tournaments in honor of the new prince. He jousted with a banner proclaiming 'Sir Loyal Heart.'"

Sir Loyal Heart! I thought of what Lady Susan had said about Anne. I also remembered overhearing Master Vives mutter to my religion tutor. He said, "Lovers are madmen who lose all reason. The king is no different since he lost his reason to Lady Anne." I had listened to the gossip but refused to believe it. How could my father have changed so much?

Salisbury paused. When she resumed, her voice quivered. "And then the child died."

I sighed. My mother had told me of the newborn prince's death. She told me of my father's heartbreak. "The king and queen mourned," Salisbury continued. "But infant deaths are common. They did not despair for long. They were young and certain to produce more children. Over the next ten years, Catherine became pregnant no fewer than ten times. Each time—except one—the infant did not live."

"And that one," I whispered, already knowing the answer.

"You, my lady," Salisbury said. "It was a time for rejoicing when you entered this world healthy and squalling."

"On the eighteenth day of February, in the year 1516," I interrupted. I was sitting up now, shivering from cold and excitement.

"Three days after your birth, I carried you from Greenwich Palace to Friars' Church. I handed you to Cardinal Wolsey for your christening. You wore a white velvet robe lined with ermine. It was so long that a countess and an earl had to carry the train. You lay on a jeweled pillow under a crimson and gold canopy. The choir sang while Wolsey made the sign of the cross over you."

Salisbury had told me this part many times, but I never tired of it. She always ended by reminding me how much my father had adored me. But until now, I had not dared to question his love. I leaned over the side of my bed. "Then why does he now ignore me? What have I done wrong?" I watched her face carefully for any sign of a lie.

Salisbury sighed wearily. "Because, Mary, you are not a boy. He believes a woman lacks the strength to rule England after his death. He fears blood will be shed. He knows the people may not accept the illegitimate Fitzroy as their king." She concluded, "Above all else, your father desires a legitimate son to inherit the throne. And he is determined to have his way."

"But I am the Princess of Wales. I am to be queen—my mother told me so. Besides, my mother has not had a child for some years. She is no longer young."

"The king will have his way," Salisbury repeated. "He will stop at nothing!" She coughed into a handkerchief. "Enough now. Sleep, dear Mary." The governess clapped her hands, awakening the servant girl to relight the candle. I lay staring at the tall shadows. This much I understood: I have disappointed my father because I am not a son. I remembered how he called me his perfect little princess. But clearly, I was not perfect after all. I was only a daughter. Perhaps that was why he had elevated Fitzroy to a position higher than mine. But an illegitimate child could not inherit the crown. So it had to be a son, a legal son. But my mother could no longer bear children. What could he do? I pondered what Salisbury had said: "The king will have his way. He will stop at nothing." Suddenly I thought of Anne Boleyn. I thought of how my father had looked at her. A cold chill ran through me.

Chapter 6: The Queen in the Shadows

The horses' hooves clattered over the frozen earth. I traveled to Greenwich Palace for Christmas with my attendants. I looked forward to a season of merrymaking with my father and mother. I tried to forget what I had heard about Lady Anne. Perhaps it was only gossip. Everything would be fine.

Even the usually calm Lady Salisbury showed a spot of color in her cheeks. Her son, Reginald Pole, was expected to return from his studies abroad. I had noticed his name often entered our conversations lately. I would smile to myself but say nothing. Yet I wondered if my mother and governess had discussed Reginald as a suitable husband for me. My betrothal to the French king had been broken. There were sometimes rumors of other suitors, but I was generally left alone and was glad of it. I was nearly twelve now, approaching a marriageable age. Something was bound to happen soon.

I had known Reginald since my childhood. He was sixteen years older than me. So like his mother in height and bearing, he resembled her even in his sharp chin and long nose. I believed him to be intelligent and good. As I rode toward Greenwich, I thought I could easily come to love him. He was deeply religious, as I was. In fact, I knew he was studying to become a priest. Priests, of course, did not marry. What a shame that the very thing that drew me to him would keep us apart. Unless he had a change of heart.

Perhaps, I thought, Reginald has been thinking of me all this time. Perhaps he has come to love me as I do him! Perhaps he has already told his superiors he should become my husband. I decided I loved him even now. God was sending me Reginald Pole! But what would my father say? Reginald was not a king. My father seemed determined that only a king would do. My excitement died before we even passed through the palace gates. My father would put an end to the plan, no matter how much I pleaded.

Once inside Greenwich Palace, King Henry summoned me. I changed from my traveling clothes and hurried to his privy chamber. My heart beat fast as I knelt before him. He greeted me with a kiss, yet he scarcely seemed to notice me. He acted as though it had been only hours since he had last seen me. He dismissed me with a wave of his hand. As soon as I reached the outer passageway, I rushed to my mother's warm embrace. But as I looked at her closely, I was shocked. Her face appeared worn and tired.

Her rich auburn hair had faded to gray. There was no true gladness in her smile. What had happened to my mother?

In that moment, I knew the rumors were true. My father no longer loves her. He is in love with Anne. My world flew apart. I wanted to cry out my pain, but I knew I must be strong. "Madam," I managed to gasp, but I could not continue. "I welcome your presence, Mary," she said gently. "Rest, and we shall talk later."

That night, I joined my parents on the dais in the Great Hall for the first court banquet. The hall was hung with sweet-smelling garlands. In the vast fireplace, flames leaped from the enormous Yule log. Long tables were laid with King Henry's finest silver and gold. Queen Catherine sat in her usual place on the king's right. Compared to other women's finery, her holiday gown seemed drab. Her headdress was old-fashioned. She looks old, I observed, my heart sinking.

In contrast, King Henry had never appeared more handsome or merry. But his happiness made me feel ill. The source of his joy was clear to everyone. At the table below us sat Lady Anne Boleyn. She wore an exquisite gown of black silk and white French lace. Her black hair curled around her pale face. My father looked at her longingly. Anne pretended not to notice his attention. In front of his entire court, the king raised his golden goblet to her. "Wassail!" (a toast to good health) he cried. Anne acknowledged him with a flirtatious smile. My throat was choked with angry tears. I could not utter a sound.

In the days after Christmas, I often sat with the queen by the fire with our needlework. I had made many of the gifts I would present on New Year's Day. I realized late that I had no gift for Reginald Pole. I had only caught fleeting glimpses of him so far. It must be a gift that expressed my affection but was also modest. In these hours with my mother, I worked on a purple silk ribbon for his prayer book. I embroidered a cross and his initials at one end, and my initials at the other. But I was distracted and uneasy. I constantly stole glances at my mother. She had said we would talk, but we had not. I wanted her to tell me what was happening, but I dreaded the news.

A few times I was alone with my mother and Salisbury, but no one mentioned Reginald. And I could not bring up the subject myself. I assumed they were as preoccupied by Lady Anne as I was. Yet no one dared speak of it. I dreaded the evening banquets. Those were the only times I saw my father. Each evening was the same. His whole attention was centered on Lady Anne. When the music began, he would dance tirelessly with her. My mother remained seated on the dais. I wondered what the other court members thought of his behavior. They seemed not to care.

Greenwich Palace was crowded. It was a great honor to be invited to court. It was easy for me to roam unnoticed through the countless chambers. Everyone always thought I was with someone else. I was an accomplished spy. As a child, I had eavesdropped on my parents' conversations. I always kept an ear open for servants' talk. Because I was a quiet girl, everyone assumed I took no interest in adult matters. They were wrong. And spying had become more important than ever. Everywhere I went, I heard whispers: "Lady Anne..." "King Henry..."

One day, I found a chance to slip into the maids' chamber. I hid myself among the gowns hanging on pegs. My heart pounded as I listened while the maids gossiped. They were talking about the large mole that grew on Anne's throat. "It is the mark of a witch," said one. "That is why she always wears a jewel on a ribbon around her neck," said another. "To disguise the place where a demon might suck." "And the extra finger on her left hand—have you noticed? Some say no one will marry her because of it." "The king seems not to mind. He seems bewitched by her." The ladies laughed, but a chill passed through me.

Later, I ran to Salisbury and repeated what I had heard. "A witch, they say," I cried. "Can it be true?" "Hush, madam!" Salisbury replied hastily. "It is nothing and better not to speak of it." It was so rare for Salisbury to use such a tone. I decided there must be truth to the slander. But who would reply to me frankly? No one. The moment I entered a room, the talk and laughter stopped.

I felt too ill to attend the New Year's Eve banquet. I could not bear another evening of watching my father with Lady Anne. But I had improved by the next day for the exchange of gifts. Lady Anne was not there, for which I was grateful. But Reginald was there, and he kissed my hand. This was the first time we could talk. And I found myself tongue-tied! I could scarcely bring myself to look at him. I had made embroidered garters for my father. He thanked me warmly and kissed me fondly. This was the first affection he had shown me. In return, I received a gold cup from my father and a silver pomander (a ball of perfumes) from my mother. Reginald's gift was a gilded spice box. It was enameled with scenes from the Book of Job's suffering. I had longed for a gift that might speak of the feeling I hoped was growing between us.

Twelfth Night, the last great feast, was a time of rowdy merriment. An enormous spiced fruitcake was set ablaze. The gentleman who found a bean in his slice would be crowned Lord of Misrule. The lady who found a pea would be his queen. The honor went to Thomas Wyatt, a handsome poet in the king's court. This seemed to please my father, until he learned that the lady was Anne Boleyn. The storm clouds began to gather. Wyatt begged to sing a song he had composed for his "queen." "Get on with it then," growled the king. As Wyatt strummed his lute, I saw his gaze was fixed on Anne. King Henry noticed, too. The storm was about to break. Rudely, the king interrupted, exclaiming, "Enough of this melancholy caterwauling!" He declared the banquet at an end.

On the eve of our departure, I roamed the palace one last time. I happened upon a group of high-ranking ladies playing cards. Dressed plainly, they mistook me for a servant. "It is common knowledge that Lady Anne came from France intending to marry young Percy," said a stout woman in yellow silk. "And she refused another man her father had chosen for her!" said a woman in green velvet. I crouched by the fire, pretending to tend the logs. "In any case," continued Yellow Silk, "the cardinal broke up the love affair. He married off poor Percy to an ugly woman." "Making Lady Anne furious, no doubt," said a third. "Oh, she said terrible things about Wolsey! She swears she will have her revenge." She continued, "Percy was not her first lover, nor her last." "Who else then?" "That handsome poet, Thomas Wyatt. He has a wife as mean as a starving dog!"

"Did you not see how the king behaved last night?" asked a new voice. "Whenever he catches Wyatt near Lady Anne, King Henry sends the poet off." "I've heard he wants to marry Anne," said another. "Marry her? But how can he? To marry her, he must first divorce Catherine." I thought I would choke. The dreadful woman in yellow silk replied, "But that is just what he intends to do. To divorce Catherine, he must have his marriage to her declared invalid. And declaring the marriage invalid means his daughter is illegitimate." The log crackled. "The Princess Mary a bastard? If a bastard, then she is no longer a princess."

That was all I heard, for I fainted, crumpling upon the hearth. When I came to, I was in my chamber with Salisbury bending over me. "Mary, what's wrong?" But I could not bring myself to utter a single word. The next morning, I gloomily prepared to depart. My father did not send for me. My mother bade me a sorrowful farewell. I wanted to ask her so much, but I could tell from her face that I must not question her. All she told me was that the king had ordered her to a manor house far from Greenwich. Before we left, Reginald Pole again kissed my hand. He told Salisbury time would not allow him to call upon us before he left for the Continent. This was yet another disappointment. Salisbury and I dragged ourselves back to Richmond through wet snow. We spoke little, each wrapped in her own heavy thoughts.

Chapter 7: A Season of Sickness and Sorrow

The church bells were silent. Crucifixes in the royal chapels were veiled in black. The forty days of Lent were nearly over. I had traveled from Richmond to the court in Greenwich for Passion-tide and Easter. I had always loved Easter, the most dramatic church celebration. But this year was different.

On Good Friday, the entire company abstained from food and drink. We watched as King Henry crept on his knees down the long aisle of Westminster Abbey. He wore a robe of brown sackcloth and sprinkled ashes on his bare head. In the past, I had been moved by my father's humble piety. This year, I knew it was false, and it sickened me.

Holy Saturday was a time of waiting. My whole life had become a time of waiting to find out what was happening to my family. One thing was clear: my parents were at war, and I was powerless. For three months, memories of my father's obsession with Anne Boleyn and my mother's sad eyes had kept me awake.

At nightfall, my maids dressed me for the Great Vigil of Easter. Last season's gown of amber velvet had grown tight across my chest. Salisbury had written to the king for an allowance for a new gown, but she received no reply. It was as if he had completely forgotten he had a daughter. I understood the reason was Anne Boleyn. People now spoke openly about his new love. There was nothing left for me.

As I was squeezed into my poor old gown, we made our way to the abbey. In the chilly darkness, we waited. Then a spark was kindled at the great door. From it, the tall paschal candle was lit, signaling the return of light. Cardinal Wolsey led the procession. Trumpets and sackbuts announced the joyous news of Christ's resurrection. The great organ, silent for forty days, swelled in massive chords. The choir of monks sang hallelujahs, but I could not share in the joy.

That night at the Easter feast, Queen Catherine appeared at the king's side. A tight smile was on her lips, but her brown eyes were sad. The king looked furious. Not even Anne's presence distracted his angry glare. When the banquet ended, my parents retired to my mother's chambers. I knew they were arguing. Everyone in the palace knew.

I pleaded with Salisbury to tell me what they argued about. At last, she relented. "King Henry demands a divorce," she said. "He claims his marriage to Catherine is invalid because it is incestuous. He married his brother's wife, which Scripture forbids." She continued, "Queen Catherine refuses. She quotes a different Bible passage where a husband's brother is commanded to marry the widow. Each of them stands fast. Henry flies into towering rages, demanding she enter a nunnery."

After one of these arguments, I found my mother hunched in her chair, exhausted. For the first time, she spoke to me openly. "Your father has lost his senses; he's mad over the goggle-eyed whore," the queen said bitterly. "He'll do anything to have her. But I will not relent. It is for you that I remain strong! I will do nothing that will jeopardize your claim to the throne." She insisted, "If I agree to your father's demands, you will be declared a bastard. That makes you unfit to inherit the throne. I will die before I agree! You must be queen, Mary, no matter the cost."

I sank to the floor by my mother's side and took her hand. "Dearest Mother, I don't want to be queen!" I cried. "Let my father do as he wishes, but let us live in peace."

Queen Catherine was on her feet in an instant. "Mary, stop this at once, I command you! There will be no weakness! You shall be queen! But we shall have to fight." She warned, "We are surrounded by enemies. Trust no one, except for Salisbury. Now go! The king has ordered me to move again, this time to the More. We must not be weakened by our separation. With God's help, we shall prevail."

She sounded so strong and brave. I knew how much she disliked the More, a gloomy hunting lodge. I kissed my mother's hand. "I will do as you command," I said, wishing I could command her pain to stop. At that moment, I hated my father. I could not forgive him for the hurt he caused my mother. Her words had terrified me.

When I returned to my chambers, Salisbury had even more frightening news. The first cases of the dread sweating sickness had been reported in London. A page brought a message from the king that I was to leave quickly. It was the only message I had from him during the entire visit. The boy who delivered it looked pale himself. Salisbury had begun to pack.

Three times in the past, the kingdom had been ravaged by the sweat. Thousands had died. The sweating sickness took strong adults in their prime. After the first symptoms, death usually followed within hours. The priests said it was a punishment for sin. As fear swept through London, roads became clogged with people fleeing. Safe on the royal barge, Salisbury and I shut our ears to the tolling church bells. If this dreadful plague is a punishment for sin, I thought, perhaps it will take Lady Anne. I felt no guilt for this wicked thought.

Scarcely two days had passed when I began to complain of a pain in my head. This was not unusual for me. But the pain worsened, and I developed a fever and a squeezing in my chest. Within hours, I tossed in my bed, moaning with pain. Poisonous sweat poured from me, and my hair lay matted on my pillow. Drifting in and out of consciousness, I was unaware of what was happening. Salisbury told me about it later.

While I lay ill, my bedchamber bustled with activity. Salisbury sat by my side, refusing to leave. My physician, Dr. Butts, paced at the foot of my bed, looking grave. He ordered me to be bled. I was so weak that I was unaware of the leeches on my arms and back. He ordered me to be wrapped in blankets with hot coals placed between the layers. He hoped the heat would drive out the fever. He ordered me to be given no food and to be kept awake. He feared if I fell deeply asleep, I would not wake again.

Wretched nights followed miserable days. Despite the efforts of Dr. Butts, I floated in a dream world, calling out for my mother. I would open my eyes to see Salisbury hovering over me, bathing my cracked lips. For more than a week, I hovered between life and death.

Abruptly, the fever broke. I called out for food and ate hungrily. I fell into a calm, dreamless sleep, woke and ate, then slept again.

"Did my mother come?" I asked.

Salisbury shook her head. "The king forbade it," she snapped.

"And Reginald?" I asked weakly.

"He returned to Rome at Ash Wednesday, madam. Have you forgotten?" I had. My legs were so weak that when I took a few steps, I nearly collapsed.

Salisbury sat by my side and read to me from Malory's *Morte d'Arthur*. It told stories of the mythical King Arthur. I lay back and listened as Salisbury's voice brought the fabled romances to life. Master Vives would never permit such idle pleasure, I thought. He would scream and snatch the forbidden book from my hands. I loved Salisbury for daring to defy him.

"Do read more, Salisbury," I begged. "But take care that Master Vives does not learn of this!"

The countess closed the book. "Master Vives has been carried off by the sweating sickness," she said. "Many here were taken, Vives among them. His soul departed a fortnight ago, while you yourself were so ill. We mourn his passing, but we thank God that you were spared."

"He's dead?" I pushed myself upright. "Master Vives is dead?"

"Yes, madam."

I sank back against my pillows. Never again to be tormented by Vives! A small bubble of relief grew in my chest, but I hid my feelings. I would confess them to the priest. "And will I have a new tutor?" I asked in a solemn voice. "Wolsey is seeing to it," Salisbury said. I sighed. In that case, my relief might not last long.

The days passed as I slowly recovered my strength. I began to take short walks. As my vigor returned, I was eager to ride again. I wanted to see my hawk, Noisette, and even more, I wanted to see Peter. I had not hunted with him since late winter.

On a warm afternoon, I slipped out of the palace and hurried to the mews. Instead of the usual activity, I found only gloom. Peter's father, the falconer's assistant, dropped to one knee when I approached. Tears sprang to the man's eyes. "I am well, Your Highness," he said. "But alas, I lost my son, Peter, to the sweating sickness. Oh, it has been a terrible time! His grave in the churchyard is still fresh."

"I am truly sorry," I managed to say, turning away to hide my own tears. Then I turned back to the falconer. "I have come to see my hawk," I said, my voice betraying my feelings. The falconer led me to the mews, where Noisette perched quietly. "She's starting her molt," he said. "Through the summer she'll just perch here and grow new feathers. Come autumn, she'll need some training to get her hunting again. That was Peter's duty. He was so good with them."

I touched the man's shoulder and moved away. "Come," I said to my ladies, "we will take roses from the palace gardens to Peter's grave." I summoned the gardener to bring a knife and a basket. He began to cut the roses, but I waved him aside. "I will do it myself." "Mind the thorns do not prick you, Your Highness," the gardener warned. One by one, I cut the fragile white blossoms. I twined the thorny stems together to form a garland. Susan and Winifred tried to help, but they quickly gave up.

When the garland was made, my hands were scratched and bleeding. "I will carry the roses to the churchyard myself," I told them. "Let one of us do it for you, madam," begged Susan. "You've been ill." But I brushed her offer aside. Clouds had drifted across the sun, chilling the air. The sky darkened; a mist began to gather.

We stopped at a gate in the stone wall and peered into the churchyard. Clods of sod lay scattered around dozens of fresh graves. I approached two gravediggers, who stopped their work. "I am seeking the grave of Peter, son of the falconer's assistant," I said. They pointed out a heap of raw earth. "There he lies," one mumbled.

The mist thickened and turned to drizzle. I lifted the garland and laid it tenderly on the mound of earth. While my ladies shivered, I knelt on the wet ground. I offered a prayer for the soul of Peter, my departed friend. As I was leaving, I darted back to the gravediggers. "And Master Vives? Show me where he was put to rest." Again they pointed. I returned to Peter's grave, plucked a single rose from the garland, and placed it on the grave of Juan Luis Vives. My prayer for the tutor's soul was brief, but my Latin was perfect.

Salisbury clucked in dismay when I stumbled wearily into the royal apartment. My petticoats were torn and muddy. I toppled into bed, my strength gone. For another week I lay listlessly among my pillows. I was well in body, but my sorrow over Peter's death wounded me deeply. On the seventh Sunday after Easter, church bells celebrated Whitsunday. This year there was no invitation to Greenwich Palace. The sweating sickness still raged in London. Death had touched every family.

My new tutor arrived. I watched from my window as he rode into the courtyard. He appeared to be a man of middle years, short and plump. His clothes were threadbare and drab. His name was John Fetherston. "I understand Your Highness has been trained in the ancient tongues," he said in Latin. I responded, also in Latin. He changed to Greek, which I handled less well, but I managed a reply. He smiled, his round cheeks reminding me of painted cherubs. I watched him suspiciously, still recovering from the madness of Master Vives.

"Perhaps we can teach one another," said the tutor, bowing over his round belly. In the weeks that followed, I waited for him to scream at my errors. But it seemed his kindly disposition matched his cherubic appearance. He did have one interesting habit. When displeased, he frowned deeply with his left eyebrow while the right one arched nearly to his hairline. It was such a curious quirk that I sometimes made a minor error just to provoke it.

Chapter 8: The King's Fury

It was late summer when the messenger arrived. I could scarcely believe what I read, though I recognized the royal seal and the king's signature. I rushed to Salisbury with the news. "My father is coming!" I stammered. "His hunting party is nearby, and he wishes to see me." Salisbury sent the cooks scurrying to prepare a feast. I summoned my mistress of the wardrobe to find me a suitable gown.

Lady Julia wrung her hands. "But madam," she said, "most of your gowns have been outgrown. The ones that can be made to fit are badly worn."

"But surely the king has sent money for new ones?"

"No, madam, none has been received," she promised, "I will do my best to dress you like a true princess."

The night before the king's visit, I slept little. This was the first time the king had come to call on me in my own palace. Always before, I had been summoned to him. By sunrise, I was dressed and ready. Lady Julia had performed miracles on my old gown of amber velvet. All morning I paced the long gallery, hoping to catch a glimpse of the procession. At last, I spotted the green-and-white pennants whipping in the breeze. At the same time, my pages raced in, breathless with news: "The king is coming! And Lady Anne!"

I was speechless. I waved the pages away and struggled to control my anger. How dare he bring Anne Boleyn with him! At that moment the countess appeared. "Madam, your father is arriving. Are you ready to receive him?"

"I'm ready to receive the king. But, Salisbury, he has brought that evil woman with him!" I cried. "Must I receive her as well?"

Salisbury gaped, openmouthed. "Lady Anne is with him? Surely not! But come, Mary. You're a Tudor. Show your courage. Let us go down."

King Henry entered the Great Hall, towering above a crowd of knights and huntsmen. With hands as cold as ice, I approached him. The crowd parted as I neared. My eyes darted around in search of Anne Boleyn.

"Ah, Mary, my pearl, my prize!" boomed the king.

Instantly I dropped to my knees. "Your Majesty," I murmured. When my father raised me, I saw only his blue eyes and mirthless smile. His face seemed unhealthily red, and he had gained weight. Still, I thought him handsome. "Welcome, Your Majesty," I said, my throat dry. "We've prepared a meal for you, but we had little notice."

"I've not come here to feast, daughter," said King Henry. "Let us talk privately while the others dine."

Trembling, I led the way to my privy chamber. What did he want to tell me? There was still no sign of Anne, but I felt no relief. I waited as the king called for bread, meat, and ale. When it arrived, he sent everyone from the room. He tore off a piece of bread and dipped it in the roast's juices. I sat perfectly still, unable to eat, fearful of what he had to say.

At last, he stared at me with cold eyes. "I will speak plainly. I am determined to divorce your mother. Scripture proves that I must." He continued, "Your mother and I addressed the court of churchmen. There is no question that I'm right! The marriage is invalid; Catherine was married to my own brother. But your mother is a stubborn woman. She walked out of the court and refused to return. I've begged her to enter a nunnery, but she refuses. Mary, your mother will not have the last word on this! I do this not for myself but for England. I must have a son, a male heir."

As my father ranted, I kept my face blank as a stone. Inside, I was in seething turmoil. *How he lies!* I though, my anger boiling. I knew everything depended upon my silence and composure. Finally, I ventured one question: "You would make me a bastard then, Your Majesty?"

Furious, the king leaped to his feet. "What difference does it make to you, Mary? You are a woman and not fit to rule England! And the people will not allow a foreigner to rule for you as your husband. You are as stubborn as your mother, and I curse you both!" King Henry pounded on the table with his fist, setting the goblets jumping. "I—must—have—a—son!" he roared.

With one sweep of his arm, goblets, plates, and everything else flew off the table. They crashed onto the floor, splashing my velvet gown. I jumped to my feet, pressing a hand to my mouth to keep from making a sound. My father stormed out. At the last moment, he turned. "Good day, madam," he bellowed and slammed the door behind him.

I stood in stunned silence, staring at the wreckage. "I am not a bastard," I whispered, my whole body shaking. That was how Salisbury found me. She summoned servants to clean up the mess. Later that day, I again watched from the gallery as the royal procession left. Riding beside King Henry was a woman on a black horse. She was dressed in black and silver, her black hair swirling loosely. Her brittle laugh drifted up to me as I angrily gripped the stone ledge.

"I am not a bastard!" I shouted after them. "I AM NOT A BASTARD!" But my words were carried away by the wind.

Terrified, I awaited my punishment. I had never made the king so furious. Not knowing what he would do to me was almost worse than knowing my fate. Salisbury tried to console me. "His anger is not with you, Mary, but for your being your mother's daughter." But that was little consolation. The days and nights passed slowly as I waited and worried. What was the worst he could do? He had already separated me from my mother. The only one left who truly mattered was Salisbury. What if the king took her away and I was left all alone?

Then a messenger from Wolsey arrived. My father had not bothered to write to me himself. I scarcely dared to breathe as Salisbury read the letter. It said I was to leave Richmond and move to Beaulieu. It was another royal palace, two days' journey east of London.

"Nothing else?" I asked Salisbury.

"Yes, madam, there is one thing more. You are no longer permitted to write to your mother or to receive letters from her."

"Not allowed to write! But how can he do this?" I cried, although I knew the answer: because he is the king.

Then Salisbury did something unusual: she put her arms around me. "We will find ways, madam," she murmured.

Thanks be to God for Salisbury! At least I still had her. But I knew in my heart that when I left Richmond, a chapter of my life was at an end. I was no longer the king's perfect pearl. And I knew exactly where to lay the blame: on Anne Boleyn. The nights grew cool. The hawks would be ready to hunt again. When the household goods had been packed, I made a last visit to the mews. A boy I did not know was sweeping the yard.

"I've come to see Noisette," I said.

The boy disappeared and returned with my merlin on his gloved fist. How beautiful she looked in her new plumage! "Will you be taking her along to Beaulieu, Your Majesty?" asked the boy. "No," I said shortly, and pulled on my hawking glove. This was a decision I had not made easily. I sounded the three-note whistle that Peter had taught me. Noisette leaped from the boy's fist and glided to mine. I felt the hard grip of her talons through the leather. "Now bring me her bells and hood."

The boy looked uneasy. "Are you planning to hunt with her now, madam? She's not lean enough yet. This one will fly away from you."

"I understand," I said. "Now do as I say." The boy obeyed.

Carefully, I unhooked the leash attached to the silk jesses (short straps) fastened around the bird's legs. Then I untied the jesses. The bird stood free on my fist. I walked out a little ways. Noisette gazed at me with her fierce yellow eyes. "Farewell, Noisette," I murmured. I raised my arm and thrust the bird into flight. The merlin spread her wings and lifted off. She circled once and flew to the top of a nearby tree.

The red-faced boy caught up with me. "You could try whistling her back," he suggested.

"No," I said. "She will not come back."

I took the bells and hood from the startled boy and walked to the village churchyard. Grass had grown thickly over the new graves. I found the one marked with Peter's name carved on a small wooden cross. I hung the silver bells upon it. "Farewell, Peter," I whispered.

Chapter 9: An Ambassador's Warning

While servants arranged my things, I explored Beaulieu. I investigated the kitchens and gazed at the Great Hall's smoky beams. I decided where Lady Susan and the others would be quartered. I also chose the small chamber for my studies with Master Fetherston. I tried not to think about my father. But at night, the sound of his angry words thundered in my ears. I also heard Anne's chilling laughter.

I worried about my mother. Salisbury had made it possible for us to send secret messages. But my mother's letters were more and more disturbing. They were troubling because of what she left unsaid.

On a chilly November day, my ladies and I were doing our needlework. Salisbury had found the chapel's altar hangings were faded and threadbare. She had my maids-in-waiting stitch a new set of linen for the altar. Salisbury herself embroidered a new lilac silk frontal for the Advent season. "We are to expect a visitor," Salisbury said. She paused to thread her needle.

I glanced up from the kneeling cushion I was stitching. "A visitor?" For a moment I thought it might be Reginald Pole. But I quickly realized that nothing could come of such a visit. "Who is it?"

"His name is Eustace Chapuys. He is an ambassador sent by your cousin, Emperor Charles."

We continued our work and waited for our visitor. Days later, in the middle of an early snowstorm, Chapuys arrived. The first time I saw him, wet snow covered his cloak, boots, and hat. "Your Majesty," said the snowy ambassador, kneeling at my feet. Melting snow dripped onto the floor.

"You are welcome here," I replied. A watery drop clinging to his red nose fell away. It was immediately replaced by another.

"Perhaps Your Highness would join me in a walk around the palace gardens?" suggested Chapuys.

I laughed. "In this weather? It is not fit for wild beasts out there! And you must be chilled from your journey."

Chapuys tilted his head. His black hair and beard were streaked with silver. His dark eyes were half hidden beneath thick brows. He seemed not to have heard me. "I would consider it a great honor if Your Highness would show me the gardens." Then he added softly, "Your mother suggests it."

I drew in my breath. "Wait for me in the garden by the chapel royal," I murmured.

Chapuys bowed deeply and left. I called for a fur-lined cloak and leather boots. I quickly made my way to the chapel royal. Dozens of candles flickered around the statue of the Blessed Virgin. I knelt and uttered a short prayer. Then I pulled up my cloak's hood and slipped out the chapel door.

I rushed to the dark figure silhouetted against the snow. "Have you word for me from my mother?" I asked.

The figure turned. "Your Highness, I beg you, be more careful," said Chapuys. "You could not have been sure it was I. Your mother is in grave danger. You may be in danger as well. Come, let us walk. Out here only the bare trees can overhear us."

Chapuys had frightening news. He spoke rapidly in French as we slowly circled the small garden. "The queen's household has spies in every corner. Cardinal Wolsey placed them there with the king's approval. Wolsey himself is in a bad situation. The pope has refused to grant King Henry a divorce, and Henry is furious. He blames Wolsey."

"Refused the divorce?" I had not heard this news, and I was elated. "That ends it, does it not?"

But Chapuys shook his head. "Henry will do whatever he must to have his way. He wants to be rid of his lawful wife so he can marry Anne. She is putting pressure on him. She wants to be queen!"

I stopped short. "Queen?" I gasped. "She wants to take my mother's place as the king's wife and queen?"

"Anne Boleyn is as ruthless as she is ambitious. She has the king dancing on a string." Chapuys took my arm, and we resumed our walk. "Your cousin Charles is concerned for your safety. He sent me as his ambassador to Henry's court. My secret instructions are to assist you and the queen. You may count on me as your friend."

We crossed our own dark footprints in the wet snow. I felt frightened, angry, and helpless. "There is more you should know, madam. The cardinal has enemies of his own. Perhaps his most dangerous enemy is Lady Anne."

"I know of her dislike for Wolsey," I said. I remembered the ladies gossiping at cards.

Chapuys raised his great, bushy eyebrows. "Ah! So madam employs spies of her own, then?"

I smiled. "Only one," I said. "Unfortunately, she cannot be everywhere at once. And since I keep her by my side, there is much she doesn't know." Now it was Chapuys's turn to smile.

We began another circuit of the garden. "Has your spy reported that Lady Anne turned the king against the cardinal?" Chapuys asked. "She convinced Henry that Wolsey is to blame for the pope's refusal. Henry already believes the cardinal is an arrogant fool. You have visited Hampton Court, Wolsey's home?"

"When I was a child my parents took me there," I said. "I don't remember much."

"I have recently come from there. Wolsey lives like a king—some say better than Henry himself. Hampton Court is filled with priceless art from France and Italy. It is far more lavish than Greenwich Palace. Anne cannot bear it. She wants him stripped of everything." He continued, "The cardinal owns nearly three hundred beds! He showed me his own bed with its gilded posts and ivory carvings. This is in addition to York Palace, his London mansion."

"I've visited York," I said. "I've seen him sit upon his golden chair."

Chapuys sighed. "I can tell you, madam, that the cardinal's silver and gold plate far exceeds the king's. His own bishops hate him. Lady Anne hates him. The king no longer trusts him. And there is another reason Henry despises him. It is an open secret that Wolsey has several illegitimate sons. This churchman has more of everything than the king! Wolsey will soon be out of power. The mystery is who will take his place. But you must be on your guard. The queen expresses great concern for you."

The mention of my mother made me feel sick with fear. "When did you last see my mother?"

"I have come directly from her. She wishes you to know her resolve is as strong as ever. She begs you to remain steadfast."

"Thank you," I managed to say. "Now, shall we return and warm ourselves?"

Later, we sat by the fire and were served a simple meal. Chapuys seemed to enjoy his. I was far too distressed to eat. His account had been horrifying. Everything I knew and counted on was changing. As much as I despised Wolsey, my father's turning on him was also unsettling. What would Anne want next?

In the following days, the ambassador tried to distract me. He coaxed me to play upon the virginals, which I had not touched in weeks. I could think of only sad songs. "Many years ago, my cousin Charles taught me to play chess," I told him. "Would you accept my challenge, ambassador?"

"Willingly, madam."

The chessboard was brought. The ivory and ebony pieces were arranged. I attacked strongly and surrendered my pieces reluctantly. The game was paused for supper and resumed the next day. At last, I had my opponent in checkmate. Chapuys smiled admiringly. "You have done well, madam. And so you shall do in the game of life. Piece by piece, you shall triumph. I believe it—so must you."

When the visit ended, the snow had melted. Chapuys rode off for London, bound for King Henry's court. He carried a letter for my father. In it, I asked forgiveness for any slight and begged to visit my mother. There was no answer, no invitation to court for Christmas, and no gift from my father. I received a set of silver spoons from my mother, but not the letter I yearned for.

I observed the holy days soberly at Beaulieu Palace with Salisbury. There was nothing to celebrate. The winter passed bleakly. In February I observed my thirteenth birthday. I was old enough for marriage, but there was no serious talk of a betrothal. I was worthless in the game of royal marriage. I felt like a prisoner in my own palace.

One day, a messenger arrived with a letter bearing Chapuys's seal. I broke the seal. "Wolsey is dead," I read. I stared into the candle flame. For my whole life, I had despised and feared Wolsey. Yet he was a last connection to my old life as my father's cherished daughter. I held the parchment closer to the candle and read Chapuys's letter. It was written in Latin. *Death must have come as a blessing. Henry ordered him out and took all his power and possessions. This was all at Anne's insistence. Wolsey was forced to give Hampton Court to the king. He was sentenced to be executed for treason, but the disgraced cardinal died before his arrest.* The letter ended: *Beware of Thomas Cromwell, once Wolsey's assistant. He is an ambitious politician, far more sinister than poor Wolsey. It is said that he has the king's ear...* I touched the letter to the flame and watched it burn. Then I hurried to my chapel and knelt before the Virgin, intending to pray for the cardinal's soul. I found that I could not. Instead, the prayers I sent up to heaven begged God's mercy upon myself.

Chapter 10: The Hard Truth From a Friend

Season followed season. I turned fifteen. There were no invitations to court.

Every few months, Chapuys traveled from London to Beaulieu. He brought me news from the king's court and of my mother. It was now almost impossible for us to exchange even secret letters. I worried about her constantly. There was always news of Anne Boleyn as well.

"The king has removed Queen Catherine from the More," Chapuys reported. "He banished her to an even more remote manor house. It is surrounded by marshlands. The rooms are small, dark, and damp. Her health is suffering." He continued, "She is allowed only a single lady-in-waiting. The king has sent away most of her servants and reduced her allowance. She must depend on loyal country people for food and warm clothing."

"Oh, my poor mother!" I cried. "Why does he treat her like this?"

"To break her will, madam," Chapuys said. "He wants to force her to agree to his demand for a divorce."

At the end of that visit, I sent a message with Chapuys to my father. I promised that all my letters to Catherine could be read. I only asked to be allowed to write. It seemed such a small thing. But there was no reply. The rare secret letters we did exchange were sent at great risk. The loyal servants who carried them were also in danger. My mother did not mention her health, although I feared for her. In one letter she wrote, "Obey the king's every command. Do not anger him. He frightens me." But it seemed everything I did angered him.

As Chapuys had predicted, the king had appointed Thomas Cromwell as his chief minister. "He is vulgar but clever," Chapuys reported. "He is more manipulative than Wolsey. Be wary of him."

And there was this report of Anne. The king had given Anne's brother, George, the title of viscount of Rochford. "The celebration was like a wedding feast," Chapuys said with indignation. "Anne was seated on a level with the king."

"As though she already wears the queen's crown!" I exclaimed.

"She already wears the queen's jewels," the ambassador informed me. "The king sent Cromwell to demand that Catherine return her jewels for Anne to wear."

"But surely my mother refused!"

"At first she did. But then Cromwell returned with the order written by Henry himself. Catherine had no choice. She surrendered her jewels. Now Anne flaunts them."

"And she flaunts them even more because they were stolen from the queen," I finished angrily.

"There is more," Chapuys told me. "Henry has taken over Wolsey's London mansion, York. It is already a splendid palace, finer than all the others. But Henry was not satisfied. He has begun adding to it. The expense is enormous! He has done all this for Anne. He says that when she becomes queen, it will be her official residence."

"Then I shall never see it!" I snapped. Even if I were invited, I would refuse to go. While I wore simple homespun dresses, he was spending a fortune on Anne. How could he have changed so much? What had she done to him? I then thought about what the ambassador had just told me. "Do you believe that Anne will become queen?" I asked.

Chapuys stroked his silky black beard. "The people will not allow it. They believe she has bewitched the king. They hate her. When she passes by, no one cheers. There is only hostile silence." He added, "Not long ago, an angry crowd of women gathered, armed with clubs and broomsticks. They cried out, 'No Anne Boleyn for us!' Anne escaped in a boat. She may not be so lucky next time. But the more she is humiliated, the more determined the king and his Great Whore become. It is you the people want, madam, and Anne knows it. It enrages her against you. So she presses the king harder than ever to marry her."

"But how can he marry her? My mother is his lawful wife!"

"Anne will make sure of it. She has staked everything on the marriage. Her temper is shrill, and her tongue is sharp. Yet she seems to control the king. He knows he must do something quickly to provide England with a future king. He is not a young man. He leans on a walking stick. But he will find a way." I had not seen my father in three years. I was dismayed by

Chapuys's report. My father, old and weak? Anne Boleyn had sapped his strength. Perhaps it was true: Anne had bewitched him.

At Beaulieu, I lived surrounded by advisers and servants who kept a respectful distance. Only the Countess of Salisbury, Master Fetherston, and my maids-in-waiting remained close. During these two and a half years of isolation, my friendship with Lady Susan finally grew. Susan taught me card games, which Master Vives had forbidden. I taught Susan to play the virginals. We made an odd pair. I had grown thin and pale, while Susan was sturdily built and ruddy-skinned. She was the one who accompanied me on my long morning walks.

Yet even as our friendship grew, a question always lurked in my mind. Was Susan also a spy? Did she report what she heard to her father, the Duke of Norfolk? Did he then pass the information to the king or to his niece, Anne?

On one of our walks, Susan confessed that she hated her own father. "He is a bully," she said. "He slaps me and pinches me. He has even threatened to kill me if I do not obey. And now he has betrothed me to the earl of Chichester. That dreadful old man with rotting teeth!" Susan kicked at a clod of dirt. "I would rather join a nunnery. Many women are happy to shut themselves in a convent. It is because they are safe there from cruel fathers and husbands."

"It would be peaceful," I agreed, thinking of my own father. I almost confessed to Susan that I, too, hated my father at times. But I did not. I could not give up hope that someday he would again see me as his precious pearl. "But surely you would miss court life," I said instead.

"Not I!" Susan insisted.

"Perhaps your father will change his mind. My father has betrothed me several times, but he always breaks it off. Indeed, I wonder if I'll ever marry." I thought of Reginald Pole. I knew he had returned to England, but I had not heard from him for many weeks.

"You'd best hope he breaks the next one," Susan said dryly. "I've heard my father has suggested marrying you to my half-brother, Ralph."

"I've heard that, too," I admitted. "I've met your brother at court a few times. At least our ages are similar."

"Age is all that's similar, I assure you," Susan said. "Ralph is vile, bad-tempered, and rather stupid. You would not want to spend a lifetime with him."

"There is an even worse rumor," I said. "That I'm to marry my own half-brother, Fitzroy." I immediately regretted letting the secret slip. "I'm not supposed to know that. I shouldn't have told you."

Lady Susan stared at me, wide-eyed. "Then let us both take ourselves to a nunnery. A life of prayer is better than enslavement to some evil-smelling wretch."

I forced a smile. "The king wouldn't permit it. And when I become queen, I can't very well rule from a convent."

"When you become queen? Mary, you'll never be queen! Don't you understand? The king will marry Anne. She will be queen, and she will give him a son. That leaves you out."

"It's treason to speak that way!" I cried, my temper suddenly flaring.

Susan whirled around and glared at me. "It's not treason, madam—it's the truth. Who makes you think otherwise? Salisbury? That strange ambassador, Chapuys? Your mother, shut up like a prisoner in a dungeon? Can't they see what is so plain to everyone else? Can you not see it, Mary?"

"I order you to keep silent!" I shouted. "I order you to get out of my sight!" I was nearly screaming, my hands pressed to my ears.

Lady Susan dropped quickly to one knee. "I beg your pardon, Your Highness," she murmured. Then she picked up her skirts and began to run back toward the palace. I started to call out for her to wait, but then I thought better of it. Lady Susan was wrong. I would be queen! But in my heart, I knew that everything Susan had said was true. I had no future. It had all been a lie.

Chapter 11: A Farewell in Disguise

The sun dipped low, and servants lit candles in each chamber. I stood by an open window, as the Eastertide weather was unusually mild. Lady Susan and Lady Winifred sat nearby with their lutes. As the sky deepened, I watched a lone, dark figure shamble along the road.

"Another wretched beggar, no doubt," Winifred observed.

The dogs began to snap and howl at the tall figure in ragged clothes. He fended them off with his staff. I looked again, more carefully. Could that be? Abruptly, I turned from the window. "Stay," I said to my ladies, and rushed out to find Salisbury.

I found the countess in the pantry. "Come," I said, and she followed me into the passageway. "It's Reginald," I whispered. "I'm sure of it. He has come disguised as a beggar. He's outside now. Oh, Salisbury!"

"I will see to it at once, madam."

I hurried back to the chamber where my ladies were. I slowed my steps and entered calmly. The maids stopped playing and curtsied. "I must change to another petticoat," I said. The maids glanced at each other but were silent. Nothing in my wardrobe felt right for this visitor. Cromwell had not sent money for clothes. Usually I dressed simply in a plain woolen kirtle. My only choice for dressing up was a blue petticoat and bodice Salisbury had made for me.

Susan helped me into it, lacing up the back. Then she combed my hair until it fell over my shoulders in a red-gold ripple. I held up a mirror and studied my image. I could see Susan's puzzled look reflected in the glass. I longed to tell her about the disguised beggar, but I could not risk it. Was Susan loyal to me? Or would she betray Reginald to her father, to Anne, to the king? To appear calm, I opened a book. I handed it to Lady Winifred. "Please read to us," I said. Presently, Salisbury joined us, looking composed.

At last, I could bear it no longer. "Have we a visitor below?" I asked Salisbury coolly.

"A begging monk, I'm told," Salisbury replied just as coolly. "The chamberlain invited him to stay the night. He is being fed with the servants.

He will pay his respects tomorrow, if the princess wishes." How aggravating! Reginald would eat with the servants while we dined separately. We could not speak of this exciting event. As we left the table, Salisbury managed to whisper, "Chapel. Ten o'clock."

The hours dragged by. I went through the motions of a normal evening, aware that Susan was watching me. At last, the maids-in-waiting were dismissed. Salisbury and I walked slowly to the chapel for our evening prayers. As we knelt, the only sound was the murmur of our voices. "Gloria in excelsis Deo..." (Glory to God in the highest). I heard the chapel door creak. "Laudamus te" (We praise thee). I felt a faint breeze and heard the latch click. "Benedicimus te" (We bless thee). Eyes closed, I listened to soft footsteps approaching. "Adoramus te" (We adore thee). I sensed a presence beside me and forced myself to remain still. Then a familiar voice joined ours. "Gratias agimus tibi propter magnam gloriam tuam..." (We give thee thanks for thy great glory).

Not until the last amen did I open my eyes. I gazed at the man kneeling beside me. Even in a beggar's ragged clothes, Reginald's piercing blue eyes were unmistakable. "Your Highness," he whispered. "Reginald," I said, reaching out to touch his hand.

He rose and kissed his mother. "It's safe to talk here," Salisbury said in a hushed voice. "Provided we do not stay too long."

"I have come to say my farewells," said Reginald. "The king has ordered me to leave England at once. He forbade me to come here, but I could not leave without seeing you. God knows when I will return. Certainly not as long as your father lives, Mary. Henry is in a rage against me. He would kill me if he could."

"But what have you done, my son?" cried Salisbury in anguish. I pressed a handkerchief to my lips, afraid I would cry out.

"I wrote the king a letter opposing his divorce. I confess my words were not mild. I wrote that Lady Anne is another Jezebel. I reminded King Henry of Jezebel's fate. She was thrown from her window, trampled by horses, and her flesh eaten by dogs."

Salisbury looked frightened. "This was not wise, my son."

"But it is the truth! Anne Boleyn is a sorceress who has bewitched the king. And Cromwell is a flatterer and a scoundrel. Henry is nearly bankrupt. He has squandered his vast fortune. Now he has given Cromwell the task of finding money. The new taxes are crushing the people. The kingdom suffers." Reginald turned his intense blue eyes on me. "I am happy to get away from court, Mary. But I am paying a price. It is taking me away from those I love best." I felt both great happiness and the deepest sorrow. But I was not prepared for what he said next.

"You may count on this," he continued. "The day is coming when the people of England will rebel. They will rise up against King Henry. They will put you on the throne as their queen, Mary."

I was too shocked to reply. The countess was on her feet at once. "Hush!" she warned. "You speak treason, Reginald. Do not ever say that to anyone." Sorrow turned to fear. Most of the chapel lay in darkness. I thought I saw a figure moving, but it might have been my own shadow. I shivered with dread. Reginald noticed and placed his rough cloak around my shoulders. It was still warm from his body.

"I am already in danger, Mother," said Reginald. "I wanted to spend time here with you." He turned to me and once more took my trembling hand. "And with you, Your Highness. But I must flee. I will go to Rome to take my final vows as a priest. You do understand, don't you, Mary? My calling is to serve God, not the king. It may be a long time until we meet again." His fingers tightened on mine. I shut my eyes, unshed tears pricking at the lids.

"May we have your blessing before you leave us?" I asked in a quivering voice.

Reginald released my hand. He laid one hand on my head and one on Salisbury's. "*Pax vobiscum*," he said. "Peace be with you." I felt the warmth of his fingers on my cold brow. I knew it was the last time I would feel his touch. "*Et cum spiritu tuo*," I murmured. "'And with thy spirit.'"

I remembered my father's boast when I was a child. "This girl never cries." But later that night as I lay in my bed, I let the tears fall onto my pillow. *He's gone*, I thought. *It is Reginald I have loved. I will never see him again. Never again.*

Chapter 12: The Usurper's Crown

The year I turned seventeen was the worst year of my life. The fault was Anne's. For six years my father had tried to divorce my mother to marry Anne. He had argued with the pope and threatened my mother. None had bent to his will. But I knew the king would not give up. He would succeed.

Anne would not give up, either. She was nearing thirty. She, too, was showing signs of age. She had to find a way to marry the king and give him a son. Or she would lose her chance to be queen. And find a way she did.

Late in the spring of 1533, Chapuys brought me the news. "Anne is expecting a child," he told me. "The king has married her. Now she will be queen." The shock was so great that I grew faint. Chapuys steadied me. "Married her! How is that possible? He's married to my mother!"

"They were married in secret in January," he said. "Anne discovered she was pregnant. For six years she has played a difficult game, tempting the king but never yielding. But she grew desperate. Becoming pregnant was the last card she had to play. She played it, and he has married her. It appears she won."

Overwhelmed, I drew away. "But does everyone know?" I stammered.

"Yes, madam, everyone knows. On Easter Eve, Anne revealed her secret. When the candles were lit, Anne stood in the place of honor. She glittered in diamonds and ermine, surrounded by dozens of ladies-in-waiting." He continued, "The priest spoke of her in his sermon as 'Queen Anne.' A sycophant! At the end, trumpets blew a fanfare. 'Queen Anne' and her small army swept out. Every knee bowed to her, as though she were a true queen."

I struggled to master the waves of emotion. "What will happen now?" I asked at last.

"Now the king must get the divorce. The child of this evil union must be able to inherit his crown."

For weeks after Chapuys's visit, I lived in torment. Then early in May, a procession of knights arrived at the palace gates. At their head rode the Duke of Norfolk, Susan's father. He demanded that everyone assemble in the courtyard. He then read the official proclamation. "Catherine of

Aragon is no longer the wife of King Henry. Therefore, she is no longer queen. From now on, Catherine will hold the title of princess dowager." I closed my eyes, willing this nightmare to stop. "It is further proclaimed that Mary, daughter of Catherine of Aragon, has been declared illegitimate. She is therefore unfit to inherit the throne." It was like a knife between my ribs.

Norfolk thrust the document under my nose so I could read the signature: *Henricus Rex*. It is a tribute to my training that I did not spit in his face. "God save the king!" Norfolk declared. His knights and most of my household replied, "God save the king!" Through the humiliating scene, I held myself rigidly silent. Norfolk was glaring at me. "Madam?" he asked.

"God save the king," I said, looking straight at him. "God save us all." I turned and walked away.

As soon as they left, I crumpled. Salisbury came to me. When Lady Susan knocked and begged to enter, Salisbury tried to send her away. But I interrupted, "Let her come." Susan rushed in, her face streaked with tears. "My father is a swine," she cried. "I hate him for what he said to you! He ignored me except to order me to London for Queen Anne's coronation. I refused."

"But you must go, Susan," I said gently. "It's not disloyalty to me or my mother. Your father commands you. It will be a festive scene. You might even have a merry time. Perhaps you will see the earl of Chichester."

Lady Susan stared at me, her mouth a shocked O. "Madam," she began, "surely—"

"Surely I'm teasing you," I said, managing a faint smile. "Do go. It will not help my cause if you refuse. Go, and listen and watch closely. Bring back news of what you see and hear."

King Henry ordered nearly everyone to attend Anne's coronation. Most of my maids-in-waiting were summoned by their fathers. There was much excitement as they prepared to leave. After they had gone, Salisbury and I were left to ourselves at Beaulieu. I brooded, thinking of my mother, whom I had not seen in six years. I confided in Salisbury the plan I had made. "While the king is busy with the coronation, I will ride to my mother. Many loyal country people will help me."

Salisbury was horrified. "Madam, this is a dangerous undertaking! The roads have thieves who will not hesitate to slit your throat. The king has spies everywhere. When he learns you disobeyed, you will both be punished. Have you forgotten his temper?"

"I have not forgotten."

"And I beg you to remember this. You must not risk your safety. Someday you shall be queen. The crown will rest upon your head. This is what your mother would say to you."

"Then I shall not go," I said unhappily. After a silence I added, "They say my mother must now be called princess dowager."

"In my heart, Catherine is queen," Salisbury said, smiling sadly. "And I will think of her as queen until that title is yours. We all have our rebellions. That is mine."

The maids-in-waiting returned, unable to hide their excitement. I sent for spiced wine while the ladies talked. I insisted on hearing every painful detail. "I was there when Anne's barge arrived at Tower Wharf," said Lady Susan. "Hundreds of boats decorated with flowers had traveled from Greenwich. The Tower guns saluted her." I remembered riding with my mother in the royal barge, her pomegranate emblem painted on its sides. "My mother's emblem—," I began.

Susan sighed. "It was replaced with Anne's. She has taken her white falcon, crowned it, and placed it on a bed of roses. Anne stayed in the Tower for two days."

"I watched Anne's procession to Westminster Abbey," said Lady Winifred. "She rode in an open litter. Her knights carried a canopy embroidered with her motto, *La Plus Heureuse*—'The Most Happy.' But when Anne passed, the crowd just stared. Her long hair was worn loose like a virgin's. Her silver gown was full over her six-month belly. The people did not even remove their caps as a sign of respect." She continued, "Along the route, the king had ordered wooden shields with the letters H and A intertwined. The crowd was silent until someone shouted, 'Look! H and A, HA-HA!' All along the route, the people took up the cry, 'Ha-ha!' as Anne passed."

"And you, Lady Winifred? Did you also cry 'ha-ha'?"

Winifred stared at her lap. "No, madam, I did not. I was with my father's people." I nodded. "I understand. I do not fault you." I turned to Lady Susan.

"And the ceremony?" I asked. My head was throbbing with another blinding headache.

"It went on for hours," Lady Susan said. "Very boring." I closed my eyes and imagined myself riding in the royal barge. Someday, I thought, it would be my turn. The streets would not be silent. There would be cheers. "Mary, Beloved Mary!" they would cry.

I came to my senses on my couch. The anxious faces of Susan, Winifred, and Salisbury floated above me. "You are ill, madam," said Salisbury, applying wet cloths to my forehead. She held a cup to my lips. "This will help you rest." I slept, but my dreams were troubled. I awoke, but the pain in my head had not stopped. The royal physician was called. The cause was a rotting tooth. He extracted a molar from my upper jaw, ignoring my screams.

My face was still swollen when Chapuys came for a rare visit. "You have heard all you care to hear about the coronation?" he asked. I nodded grimly.

"There is more bad news for the king," Chapuys continued. "The pope has again refused to grant a divorce. He has declared Henry's marriage to Anne invalid. In the eyes of the church, the baby to be born will be illegitimate." I suppressed a smile. "Another bastard," I said.

Chapter 13: A Daughter's Birth, A Father's Rage

The king's order was clear. As the current heir, I was required to witness the birth of the new heir. I was to leave for Greenwich Palace at once. The Countess of Salisbury was not to go with me. Twisting her handkerchief, Salisbury paced my bedchamber, getting in everyone's way.

"Your worry is useless," I told her. "What can Anne do to me in front of so many people? At least he still recognizes me as the heir."

"You don't understand, madam," Salisbury cried impatiently. "You will be in danger every moment. What if Anne orders her guards to assault you?"

"Rape me? Why would Anne have me raped?" My hands began to shake so badly I nearly dropped my gown.

Salisbury fell to her knees, her hands lifted in appeal. "Please listen, Mary! Once your virginity is lost, Parliament will declare you 'ruined.' You will be forbidden to inherit the throne, no matter what happens. This will make the crown even more secure for the child about to be born."

I sank down beside her. A trickle of cold sweat ran down my back. "You don't realize that Anne is like the king," Salisbury wailed. "She will stop at nothing. I will worry myself to death until you are safely back."

I had to resist my fear. "There is nothing you can do, dear Salisbury," I told her, helping her to her feet. "Nor I. We must have courage." But I felt anything but courageous.

I traveled to Greenwich with only one manservant and two of my maids. I would have chosen Susan and Winifred. But I had been told they must stay behind. I was also ordered to travel in a plain, closed litter so I would not be recognized. This was to ensure that none of my loyal supporters would rally to my cause.

This was my first time in the palace in nearly five years. I was shocked to realize how far I had fallen. Five years earlier, I was the Princess of Wales, with all the honor of my rank. Now I was nothing, no better than a servant. I was not wanted, but tradition required my presence. It was also a chance for Queen Anne to show her power over me.

When we arrived, my ladies and I were given poor rooms in a remote part of the palace. I inspected the small bed with its rough coverlet and lumpy mattress. The tallow candles in the pewter holders were smoky, not clean-burning beeswax. I was hungry but was immediately summoned to the queen's chambers. "I shall call on Lady Anne after I have refreshed myself," I told the messenger. "Her Majesty the queen commands you to pay your respects at once," the servant insisted. I followed him to the queen's chamber of presence.

Since her eighth month of pregnancy, Anne had been required to stay in these rooms. A few waiting women were tasked with keeping her entertained. Tapestries covered every window and even the ceiling. The chamber was oppressively dark and stifling. Anne reclined on a couch piled with silk pillows. Behind her, oak doors opened to an inner chamber. In that second room stood a magnificent bed. I recognized it at once—it was my mother's. My father had given it to her when I was born. Now it would be the bed where the next royal birth took place. My mother's bed! How dare she? How dare my father! From Anne's bloated and sallow appearance, the birth was near.

"So," Anne said in a shrill voice, "Lady Mary has arrived."

I stood perfectly still. *Lady Mary!* Not "Princess Mary," but a title that was no title at all. I might as well have been the daughter of the lowest baron. Anne's black eyes glittered in her pale face. "Have you no manners?" she demanded. "Then we shall have to teach you some! Kneel!"

I hesitated. This was the first time Anne and I had come face-to-face since my betrothal to the French king. I was only a child then and understood nothing. My greatest fear at that time was being forced to marry the ugly King Francis. Now, at the mercy of this wicked woman, I wondered if my life would have been better had I married him. Slowly, I sank to my knees.

Anne glared at me. "I have only contempt for you, Mistress Mary. You and your wretched, scheming mother. You are nothing but a bastard, a mistake! The king's mistake. But now he has corrected his error." She stroked her huge belly. "His one true heir lies here with me. Within days, the future king of England will be born. And you shall be his servant." She continued, "I think that will be a good lesson for you. Changing his napkins and cleaning his messes will teach you your place."

"And if it is a daughter, madam?" I asked. I immediately regretted my boldness. It was a mistake as soon as the words left my mouth. A silver goblet flew past my head and clattered to the floor. Red wine splashed everywhere. I scarcely blinked. "It is a son! It is a son!" Anne screeched. A golden pomander sailed by and struck the wall. "The physicians have predicted it! The astrologers have studied the stars! I shall bear the king his son and heir!"

I remained on my knees, my jaw clamped shut. "Get out of my sight!" Anne cried. I rose, trembling, and turned to leave. "Do not turn your back on the queen!" A sharp pain held my head in a tightening vise. Slowly, I turned to face Anne and backed out of the room.

Sprawling exhausted on the lumpy mattress, I asked God why He was punishing me. I had sent a message to my father announcing my arrival, but there had been no reply. Later, I tried to hear mass in the chapel royal but was barred by the king's guards. They did not recognize me and laughed when I told them who I was. I passed the night restlessly, tormented by another fierce headache.

Every day, Anne sent for me. She commanded me to stand behind her couch, sometimes forcing me to kneel until I thought I would collapse. I had to fill her goblet, fetch her books, and rearrange her cushions. The most disgusting moment was when Anne insisted I help her to her pewter chamber pot. I then had to carry out the waste. The only thing that allowed me to endure these insults was my burning hatred. It gave me strength when I thought I would faint.

During this time, I saw my father only once. He entered the chamber as I was leaving on one of Anne's errands. I was stunned by his appearance. He had grown fat, and his blue eyes seemed to have shrunk. He startled me by greeting me warmly. "Ah, Mary, my pearl!" he said, embracing me. Instantly, Anne's imperious voice called from her chamber. The king's mood changed at once. His smile vanished, and he pushed me away. He left hurriedly, and I noticed he was limping. A lump of anger sat hard in my stomach. It was anger at my father, at Anne, and even at God.

I returned to my old habit of spying. At first, I was offended that few in the palace recognized me. But then I found that anonymity gave me freedom. I could roam the palace almost at will. One day I stumbled upon the chamber where the king's courtiers were drinking and playing cards. They paid me no attention as I pretended to trim the candlewicks. I listened to their conversations. "The king has tired of her. She is no longer his mistress—she is his shrew." "The queen accuses him of having another mistress." "Is it true?" "The king denies it." I heard them laughing as I left the room.

After three weeks of this horror, I was awakened before dawn. I was summoned to the birthing room; the queen's labor had begun. I dressed hastily and hurried to the chamber. In the inner room, Anne lay on my mother's magnificent bed. The air was festive and excited. Frightening metal instruments were laid out nearby. The queen's ladies bathed Anne's brow and gave her sips of wine. Someone played a lute. With each pain, Anne grimaced and groaned. As it subsided, she cried, "Tell the king his son is coming!"

The day wore on, and Anne's labor continued. Everyone was weary. I was not allowed to leave her apartments. I slumped in a chair, dozing as the hours passed. At first light on Sunday, September 7, 1533, Anne's aunt, Lady Shelton, shook me roughly. "On your feet, lazy! The queen is giving birth to the king's son."

I followed Shelton into the inner chamber. Anne lay surrounded by physicians and midwives. Shelton pushed me into a place near the foot of the bed. I was shocked by what I saw. There was blood everywhere. Anne's hair was drenched in sweat. "Tell the king his son is born!" she shrieked. With one last heave, the baby slipped into the world. "The next king of England," Anne murmured. "I have done it at last." I had only a glimpse of the baby as it was handed to a nurse. That one glimpse was enough to tell me everything. The baby was a girl.

The room fell silent except for the newborn's cries. The physicians hurried to tend to Anne. The others exchanged worried glances. Exhausted, Anne seemed to sense something was wrong. "Why are you silent?" she demanded. "Why are there no cheers for the future king?"

"Madam," the head physician ventured, "the infant is a girl. You have given the king a new princess. A fine, healthy daughter." I stepped back from the bed, away from the wrenching sobs. Anne had risked everything, and she had lost. But I knew the game was not yet over.

Midwives bustled around, removing the bloody linens and freshening the bed. They placed the swaddled infant in the crook of Anne's arm. I stepped wearily into the outer passageway. I knew from the noise that the king was on his way. I slipped back into the antechamber and lost myself in the crowd. Word had spread, and anxious whispers rippled through the room. "The king is threatening to execute the physicians who promised him a son," I overheard one lord say. "He had already prepared announcements of a prince's birth," said another. "Now he must prepare new ones."

Nerves were on edge. Everyone feared becoming the target of the king's fury. I moved to the back of the crowd. "The king is coming. Make way for the king!" King Henry strode in. All dropped to their knees, but he brushed past us. I recognized the rage in his set jaw. He stalked into Anne's chamber, and the door closed. I escaped back to my gloomy quarters. I lay down on the bed, still dressed. I drifted in and out of troubled sleep.

Later that day I went to the Great Hall for supper. The gossip had spread. I sat at the table with the lesser courtiers and maids. "They say Queen Anne is distraught," reported one matron. "She continually begs the king's forgiveness." "Aye, I've heard it myself," replied her friend. "So far he has treated her kindly. But she knows if she fails to give him a son, she is finished." *Finished!* My head bent over my poor meal. I pondered what this could mean for me. If Anne was truly finished, perhaps I still had a chance to be loved again by my father. But I did not feel glad. I knew the fight was far from over. Instead, I felt afraid.

Chapter 14: Stripped of a Title, Made a Servant

There was no way out. Anne had ordered me to attend the christening of the new princess. The three-day-old infant would be named Elizabeth. Though disappointed, King Henry had ordered a grand celebration. I wondered what I should wear. Surely the king would be shamed if I appeared in a shabby gown. The day before, I sent a servant to explain the problem to Cromwell. His reply came back: "Do not worry, madam. All eyes will be on the new princess. Your clothing is of interest to no one."

Dressed in Salisbury's old, cracked silk gown, I walked far back in the procession. I was behind the nobles and their richly dressed ladies. Cromwell was right; no one noticed me. I was both relieved and resentful. That evening, the sky above London glowed red from a thousand torches honoring Princess Elizabeth. A few days later, Elizabeth was also proclaimed Princess of Wales in a splendid ceremony. I was not invited. The infant had been given my title.

That evening, as I sat at dinner, Anne's uncle, the Duke of Norfolk, rose to his feet. He read from an official document. "Elizabeth, Right High, Right Noble, Right Excellent, and Powerful Princess of England, is hereby proclaimed Princess of Wales." There was a flourish of trumpets. The company cheered. The women seated near me turned their eyes toward me. I stared straight ahead, using all my self-control to hide my hurt and anger. What were they thinking? Did they feel sorry for me? Or did they, beneath their servile smiles, hate Anne and pray for her death as I did?

In all the weeks I spent at Greenwich, I spoke with my father only once. I had no wish to speak with him again. The morning after Elizabeth was given my title, I decided to leave for Beaulieu. Within hours, Cromwell gave his permission. I wished I had my own horse; it would have been faster. Instead, I had to make the journey in an uncomfortable, closed litter. As we clattered through the gates of Beaulieu, I threw back the curtains. The countess rushed out to meet me, looking tired and distraught.

"You have a visitor, madam," Salisbury said. "Norfolk arrived just an hour ago. He must have passed you on the road."

"I did not see him," I replied. "By Cromwell's order, my curtains were drawn. Where is he now?"

"In the royal apartments, madam. With his daughter, Lady Susan."

I rushed to my audience chamber. I found Lady Susan, tearful and sniffling, kneeling before her father. His hand was raised as though he was about to strike her. "Lord Norfolk," I said sharply. The duke swung around and scowled at me. His reptilian eyes gleamed. "Lady Mary," he said, inclining his head slightly. I recognized the insolence in his failure to bow. I heard the sneer in his voice. He had pointedly not called me princess.

"How pleasant to have a visit from you," I said coldly, ignoring the insult.

"This is not a social visit, miss. By the king's orders, your claim to the title of Princess of Wales is revoked. You are a bastard. None may address you as princess. To do so is treason." He continued, "You are now to be addressed only as Lady Mary. I shall inform your household. I need not remind you that treason is punishable by death. As the king's bastard, your rank is lower than my daughter's." He glanced at Susan, cringing in a corner.

Summoning all my self-control, I remained rigid. "I shall send a letter to my father immediately, asking for a correction."

Norfolk laughed harshly. "It will do you no good. And I have not finished. You are to hand over the jeweled coronet of the Princess of Wales. You are to leave Beaulieu, which the king has given to Queen Anne's brother. You are ordered to go to Hatfield. The queen has appointed you as a waiting woman to Elizabeth, Princess of Wales. None may accompany you. You are now a servant and are entitled to no servant of your own."

My self-control deserted me. As I gasped for breath, Lady Susan suddenly leaped to her feet. "How dare you?" she shrieked, flinging herself upon her father. "How dare you speak this way to the princess?" The duke struck Susan hard with the flat of his hand. The blow sent her spinning across the chamber against a table. She crumpled to the floor. "You fool!" her father spat, standing over her. The blow had split her lip, and blood oozed from the cut. "You have just committed treason. You have also gravely insulted your father. Do you not understand I have the power of life and death over you?" The duke kicked at Susan, but she scuttled away. Abruptly, Norfolk turned and left. I stared at the thin trickle of blood on Susan's chin. I wanted to comfort her, but I felt as though all my strength was gone.

Completely numb, I watched as servants packed my possessions. Salisbury, on the other hand, seemed frenzied. I half-listened as she railed against the king, the queen, and Norfolk. "Contemptible!" Salisbury cried. "I told Norfolk I would go with you and pay for servants from my own purse. But he laughed at me! He told me, 'It is you, countess, who has made Lady Mary so stubborn. Perhaps away from your influence she will learn to bend her will to the king's.'" She suddenly permitted herself a thin smile. "What he does not realize is that all your stubbornness is a gift from your father."

The packing did not take long. The coronet was gone. All my jewels, furs, and silver and gold plate were left behind. My bed was to remain for the viscount and his wife. All the symbols of my life as a princess were stripped away. What was left? I was allowed only a few shabby gowns, a woolen cloak, and some personal treasures. There was the enameled box from Reginald, a jeweled cross from my mother, and the book of hours from Wolsey. I had my lute from my father and the embroidered hood from my hawk. At least Noisette was free. I stared with dull eyes as servants fitted everything I truly prized into one small trunk.

Most of my ladies-in-waiting were to stay at Beaulieu. Lady Susan was to be married in November. On a gray Thursday morning, a guard arrived to escort me to Hatfield. I went to bid farewell to my ladies. Susan was unusually calm. Her lip had healed, and the bruise on her cheek was fading. I sat beside her and took her cold hand. "I believe you have been my true friend," I said. "I am grateful."

Susan nodded, her large blue eyes meeting mine. "I never thought our lives would be like this," she said sadly. "If I had the means or courage, I would take my own life."

"No, Susan," I whispered. "We must prevail. Someday I shall be queen, and you shall stand by my side." I kissed her on the cheek. But suddenly, Susan's calm left her. She threw herself, weeping, upon my breast. "I shall never see you again, Mary!" she sobbed. "I feel it in my heart."

I had to be strong for both of us. "Don't speak foolishly," I said with a coldness I did not feel. I returned her embrace and whispered, "Be brave, dear Susan." Then I hurried away, my legs shaking.

I met Salisbury in the passageway. "They are waiting, Mary," she said. The governess who had taught me courage was herself composed. "I know. I am ready."

Norfolk had allowed me two servants—one old woman and one young and clumsy. The rest of my loyal servants had gathered in the courtyard to say goodbye. The women were openly weeping. I approached each one and murmured, "God bless you." I believed that if I kept moving, I would get through this. The last to bid me farewell was Salisbury. The countess, sobbing now, swept me into her embrace. I thought my heart would burst. I held back my tears, trembling. But once I climbed into the litter and the curtains were drawn, I surrendered to a storm of weeping.

Chapter 15: A Servant to the Princess

At Hatfield Palace, I found a flurry of preparations. The household was getting ready for Princess Elizabeth's arrival. New furnishings, tapestries, and silver plates were everywhere. The queen's aunts, Lady Alice Clere and Lady Anne Shelton, supervised the work. Lady Shelton, with her crow-like voice, was in charge of the royal infant. Lady Clere ruled over the rest of the household.

I was sent to a chamber near the royal nursery. Hatfield was a charming country manor, but my room was cramped and gloomy. There were a few wooden pegs for my clothing and a rough table for my books. The mattress was stuffed with straw that leaked from a rip. The thin woolen coverlet was full of moth holes. My two servants, old Nell and young Bessie, shared a pallet on the floor. All three of us would eat with the lesser maids in the Great Hall.

Lady Shelton outlined my duties. "Napkins!" she cried in her harsh voice, grinning through gapped teeth. "The queen herself has ordered it. You are to change the princess's dirty napkins whenever she soils them. You and no one else, Lady Mary," she added with scorn.

I walked to the Great Hall for dinner with my stomach already churning. It seemed everyone was mocking me. The ladies-in-waiting swept past me, laughing and whispering. They sat together at one end of the long table, looking at me. I sat alone at the other end with Nell and Bessie. For the first time in my life, I had no tasters to check my food for poison. I nibbled uneasily and finally pushed my plate away. The servers treated me with deliberate rudeness. They did not refill my cup of ale and once even tipped it over. That night, I tried to sleep, but my chamber was cold. I slept wrapped in my cloak, when I could sleep at all. I tried to pray, but I could not. It seemed God had forgotten me.

I had been at Hatfield for less than a month when Princess Elizabeth arrived. She was bundled in ermine and carried in the royal litter by Lady Shelton. Shelton immediately ordered me to change the royal napkin. I had no idea how to do this. It was soon clear that Shelton did not either. Elizabeth was wailing loudly. Then a servant showed me how to remove the soiled cloth and replace it with a clean one. By now, Elizabeth was flailing her fists and pumping her legs. Her face was red and furious.

"Loo la loo," I sang softly to calm her.

The baby stopped screaming and hiccupped. She stared up at me with bright eyes. I managed to get the napkin wrapped and secured. Only then did Elizabeth smile, a smile of pure innocence. In spite of myself, I smiled back. My heart opened just a crack.

I was approaching my eighteenth birthday, surrounded by enemies. A stream of orders arrived from Anne. She insisted her baby daughter be given every luxury. Night and day, I was reminded of my lower status. I had to walk behind the princess. I could not leave a room until she had been carried out first. And the number of wet and smelly napkins did not decrease.

My headaches worsened. Sometimes they were so fierce that I could not get out of bed. Then Shelton would shout for me and order me out. "Do not cross me, miss!" Shelton howled. "I will have you beaten for your insolence. I may beat you myself!" My only defense was silence and obedience. Shelton threatened me often, but so far she had not struck me. I had no privacy at all. My letters were ripped open and read. Someone was rummaging through my private things. The hinge on my enameled box was broken. A page from my book of hours was torn. All of this was to let me know I had nothing—and no one—to call my own.

On the eve of my birthday, I received two pieces of news. First, Nell and Bessie were being sent away. Now I would have no one to help me. But the second piece of news was much better. Princess Elizabeth was to have a new head nursemaid, Lady Margaret Bryan. Bryan had been my own nursemaid when I was an infant. She had taught me my ABCs and how to eat with a spoon. I remembered her with deep affection.

When Bryan arrived, I rushed to greet my old friend. I was aching with loneliness. Bryan had grown round as a pudding. Her skin was wrinkled, and her hair had turned nearly white. But as I reached out to her, Bryan scowled and turned away. "You are nothing more than a servant now, Lady Mary," Bryan said sternly. "Mind you do not try to rise above your station and seek favors."

I was stricken. I could not believe my beloved nursemaid had spoken so harshly. Then Bryan turned to Clere and Shelton. She announced that by the queen's order, I would now take instructions directly from her. "I am not past slapping Lady Mary when she deserves it," she assured them. "And perhaps also when she does not." Shelton and Clere smiled cruelly. Stung with humiliation, I struggled to hide my feelings.

Late that evening, the door of my room swung open silently. I lay still, hardly daring to breathe. A hooded figure loomed in the doorway. Perhaps this was the attack Salisbury had feared. I had taken to sleeping with a heavy candlestick by my side. I furtively reached for it. My fingers curled around the candlestick, and I waited. The door swung shut.

"Princess Mary!" Bryan whispered. She swept off her hood and dropped to her knees. "I beg you to forgive me. I came as soon as I could. I know I am being watched. I am forced to speak to you harshly."

I leaped from the bed and threw my arms around the old nursemaid. "Oh, Bryan! You have taken a great risk. And it's treason to call me by my title! The palace crawls with the queen's spies."

"And so we must enlist spies of our own. I am here because of my nephew, Sir Francis Peacham. He is a great favorite at court, although he despises the queen." Bryan explained, "One of the queen's ladies is in love with my nephew. To please him, she persuaded the queen to send me to care for the princess. I fear there is little I can do to help, except to be your friend. But Francis will be our eyes and ears in the queen's court."

"I am grateful to you both," I said.

"I must warn you," Bryan continued. "I shall continue to scold you before others, perhaps even slap you, to avoid suspicion. Now, I have stayed too long." We embraced again. "Courage," she whispered, and disappeared into the shadows.

Chapter 16: The King's Oath, A Daughter's Defiance

Shelton herself triumphantly delivered the news. "King Henry has declared himself supreme head of the church in England," she announced. "He demands that everyone sign a double oath. It acknowledges that he is head of the church. It also accepts that his children by Anne will inherit the throne. The penalty for refusing is a traitor's death." She leered at me. "Do you understand, Lady Mary?"

I understood. Signing meant admitting I was a bastard. "I will not sign," I said, much more calmly than I felt. I dared not think what refusing would mean.

"The king will have you beheaded!" Shelton roared. "My niece the queen has threatened to have you poisoned. I heard it from her own lips!"

"I will not sign," I repeated.

Instead, I wrote a letter to King Henry. "You are my father and my king," I wrote. "I pledge myself obedient to you in every way but one. I am your lawful daughter, born of your lawful union with my mother, Catherine." I signed it *Mary, Princess*, the title I was forbidden to use. Then I waited, terrified but determined.

No reply came from the king. Instead, Anne sent a message. She requested that I visit her and pay her the honor due a queen. "By such a large yet small act," Anne wrote, "I can guarantee you will once again enjoy the king's favor." Furious, I tore her letter to bits. I scribbled a hasty reply. "I know of no other queen in England than my mother, Queen Catherine. Her only shall I honor."

All of this caused Bryan great anguish. "I beg you, madam, submit to the king's will. Acknowledge your illegitimacy and live!"

"I cannot," I said quietly. "It is God's will that I reign someday."

"You can't rule if you are not alive, Mary."

"God will protect me," I said, hoping it was true.

Then Sir Francis smuggled a letter to me from Chapuys. He warned, "If you do not submit, you may find yourself imprisoned, even tortured. Anne is determined to put down what she calls 'that proud Spanish blood' in your veins." Still, I refused to sign. So it was not a surprise the night the guards came for me. They burst into my chamber and dragged me from my bed. Shelton was with them, her eyes glittering. Despite my terror, I did not scream or cry out.

The cell door clanged shut behind me. "You shall stay there until you lose that stubbornness," Shelton shouted through the grating. The cell was in the bowels of Hatfield Palace. I groped through the pitch darkness. My prison was five paces in one direction and three in another. I bumped into a rude plank and stumbled over a slop pail. As my eyes adjusted, I could see a small grate in the wooden door. Light from a torch in the passageway filtered through. I crept to the plank and sat on it. The cell was cold, and I had no shawl.

Surely they would not let me die here. That would cause too much scandal. If I were to die, it would have to be something subtle, like poison. It could then be announced that I had died of natural causes. But they might torture me. I feared torture more than death. How long could I hold out? I tried to pray. I believe God heard me, because I became calm. I waited, and God waited with me.

I do not know how many days passed. Then a key clanked in the lock. The heavy door was thrown open. "You have a visitor," Lady Shelton barked. I stumbled after her, unwashed and untidy. Suddenly I was thrust into the bright light of an unfamiliar apartment. A gentleman waited for me. It was Norfolk.

"Lady Mary," he said sourly. "I am sure my visit is no surprise."

"No good surprise, at any rate," I snapped, though inside I was sick with fear.

"Your wicked tongue may someday cost you your head," Norfolk observed. "I am here to have you swear the double oath. When you are ready, I shall call for a Bible and a pen."

My throat was parched. My head roared, and my eyes burned. "There is no need for a Bible or pen, sir," I said hoarsely. "I shall neither swear nor sign."

Norfolk's eyes were nearly popping from his red face. "By God!" he shouted, slamming his fist on the table. "If you were my daughter, I would not tolerate such stubbornness! I would knock your head against a wall until it was as soft as a baked apple!"

I felt my insides heave. Bitter bile rushed into my mouth. I thought I would faint. "I will not sign the paper, and I will not swear the oaths," I repeated. Norfolk stared at me, then stomped out. I remained where I was, quaking, until Shelton found me. "Look at you! A pretty sight! No wonder you have no husband!" I expected to be sent back to my cell. Instead, she just shooed me away. I stumbled back to my chamber and resumed my duties with Elizabeth.

I passed a nervous fortnight. I was afraid to eat and afraid to close my eyes at night. Elizabeth's cries and laughter were unbearable. Then I received another visitor. This time it was Cromwell. He was seated and did not rise when I entered. "Lady Mary," he began in a greasy tone. I noticed how much he resembled a toad. Beads of sweat dropped onto his doublet.

"You wished to see me," I replied.

"Sit down, won't you?" Cromwell continued. "It will make our conversation more pleasant." I remained standing. A servant poured spiced wine. I refused mine. "You wished to see me," I repeated.

Cromwell sighed deeply. "Stubborn, stubborn, stubborn," he murmured. He leaned forward. "Lady Mary, listen well. You must renounce your claim to the title of princess. It is the king's will. You and your mother must yield. There is no other way."

I met his stare. "I will not."

"The king will break your resolve if he has to break your neck to do it," Cromwell said.

"The king will do as he wishes. I will not sign."

Cromwell leaned back and drank deeply. "In some ways I admire you," he said. "But you are a fool, Lady Mary. And you will surely die for it."

Chapter 17: Whispers of a New Queen

During the long, wet summer of 1534, Sir Francis Peacham sent us bits of gossip. Anne was trying to distract the angry king with a series of elaborate banquets. Sir Francis was often asked to perform and find other entertainers. There were rumors that the queen was pregnant again. But when no pregnancy was evident, Anne's temper grew more violent and unpredictable.

One victim of Anne's spite was Susan, now the Countess of Chichester. Susan was visibly pregnant. The sight of a healthy young woman carrying a child sent Anne into a rage. "She threw at me everything she could lay her hands on," Susan wrote in a letter that reached me unopened. "Fortunately, her aim is poor. The objects fell harmlessly—harmless to me, if not to themselves, all smashed or dented." I remembered the goblet and pomander Anne had thrown at me. I was not amused when I was the target. But Susan had a humorous way of putting things. "Since she could not strike me, she banished me. So here I am, away from court and—happily, if briefly—from my noble husband. He resembles nothing so much as a pet marmoset. At least I joyfully anticipate the birth of my child."

I read the letter several times until I knew it from memory. I wished I could keep it to read again when I needed cheering. But it was not safe. I burned the letter in a candle flame. I dropped the gray ash out of my narrow window. I watched the flakes drift into the bleak courtyard below.

On one of the few August days when the sun broke through, Bryan and I took little Elizabeth for a walk. The child was nearly a year old and had just learned to walk. She was curious about everything and seemed to be everywhere at once. Elizabeth had our father's red-gold hair and her mother's black eyes. She was charming and adorable. But she had also inherited her parents' shifting temperament. She often changed from happy to furious in an instant. I refused to call her princess, but I did call her my sister. Though I had not wanted to love this child, who now had everything that was mine, she was creeping into my affections. As Bryan and I talked softly, Elizabeth toddled toward me with a flower. She reached up to pat my cheek tenderly. I could not close my heart to her.

"The queen has been arguing with the king more than ever," Bryan said quietly. "Anne insists a soothsayer told her that as long as you and your mother live, she cannot conceive a son. She urges the king to have you both murdered. She is relentless." As we watched, Elizabeth lurched into a bed of violas and began pulling at the flowers. Her fists full, she laughed and tried to run from the maidservant chasing her. But when the little princess lost her balance and tumbled, her laughter instantly turned to a tearful roar.

"The king is nearly driven mad by her," Bryan continued. "There are other rumors that the king has taken a new mistress. It is one of the queen's ladies. So Anne tries even harder to hold on to the king. She knows that if she does not soon give him a son, she will lose everything."

"The sooner the better," I muttered. "She had no right to him in the first place."

"Fool!" Bryan cried suddenly. She boxed my ear so hard that I whimpered in real pain. "You are supposed to be looking after the princess, not standing there like a post!" she shouted. My ear pounding, I ran toward Elizabeth, who was red-faced with fury. As I did, I noticed that several of Cromwell's spies had appeared. How long had they been there? Instantly Elizabeth stopped crying and ran straight into my arms. I dried her tears and returned her kisses.

Anne seldom called for Elizabeth to be brought to her at Greenwich. But for her daughter's first birthday, Anne planned a splendid celebration. I was commanded to attend. I stood with the other servants in the Great Hall of Greenwich Palace. I watched as a roasted peacock with a gilded, flaming beak was carried in. A fanfare of trumpets and sackbuts announced it. Seated on the royal dais beside King Henry, Anne was dressed in black as usual. Her hair was caught in a gold net beneath a blazing coronet. Even from a distance, the queen appeared more pale and thin than ever. Between courses, King Henry carried Elizabeth around the Great Hall on his shoulder. I remembered that he had once shown me off with the same pride. He gave no sign that he saw me. The memory, combined with my current situation, plunged me into sadness. I only wanted the evening to end so I could escape.

"The king is coming tomorrow for a visit to Princess Elizabeth," Shelton announced a few weeks later. She addressed Bryan as if I were not there. "Lady Mary is to be locked in her chamber during the king's stay. It is best if he does not see her. I have heard more talk that he will have her beheaded if she refuses to swear the oaths." Only then did she seem to notice me, giving me a sour, toothy smile. My heart beat rapidly, and I struggled to hide my trembling. Perhaps Shelton was telling the truth.

"And so she shall be," Bryan declared, seizing my arm. "Stop struggling!" Bryan hissed, dragging me down the gloomy passageway. "I'm trying to help you." When we reached my chamber, Bryan whispered, "It is better if you are here. These are Anne's orders. At least you will be safe with a guard at your door." She then left me alone.

Locked in my chamber, I passed a long and sleepless night. I listened to the sounds of the palace and the murmur of the guards outside. The next day, I heard trumpets announcing the king's arrival. I waited with a pounding heart to learn if he might send for me. But if he did, what then? Would he order my death? Hours later, trumpets signaled his departure. Still, I hung in an agony of suspense. I hoped Bryan would come to release me and bring me news. Instead, it was Shelton who appeared. "You have a visitor," she said, her cold eyes glinting. Another visitor? My father had gone. Who, then? In a panic, I wondered if it was Norfolk or Cromwell, come to haul me to the Tower. Wordlessly, I followed Shelton to my fate.

I nearly wept with relief when I found the visitor was my former tutor, Master Fetherston. I had not seen him for two years. The look of surprise and concern on his cherubic face showed me how much I must have changed. For his part, Master Fetherston had changed little, except to grow even plumper. "Lady Mary," he said, arching one eyebrow while frowning with the other. I understood his curious gesture. He was forced to address me this way and did not do so willingly. A half dozen maidservants stopped to listen.

"Master Fetherston," I said, "I am so delighted to see you." Then, thinking quickly, I continued, "And I am so pleased to finally have someone to speak Latin with. My skill in that language has weakened from disuse." I smiled. "Thank God you are here," I said, switching to Latin but keeping a false, bantering tone. "I am in terrible danger."

Master Fetherston nodded wisely. "Yes," he replied in English, "I see you do need practice." We continued our conversation in Latin, to the clear annoyance of the listening servants. "I have brought a letter from your friend Chapuys. He understands your danger and has sought help from your cousin, Emperor Charles."

"Have they devised a plan to help me?" I asked.

"The ambassador has a scheme, but he must wait for a sign from the emperor. I warn you—it will be difficult."

"I will do anything to escape. Anything!" I said, too passionately. Alerted by my tone, the serving maids turned to stare. The tutor immediately switched to English. "My dear Lady Mary," he chided, "you must obey your father and yield to his wishes. You must sign the papers and take the oath. It is your duty, Lady Mary." I knew he said this for the eavesdroppers, but it stung nonetheless. I turned my face away. Then I felt his hand on my arm. He slipped something into my sleeve. Master Fetherston bowed briefly and was gone.

I rushed back to my chamber and pulled a tiny folded paper from my sleeve. I held it close to a candle. Chapuys had written in handwriting so small I could barely read it. At first, I deciphered only a few words. My poor eyes watered and my head throbbed. At last, I managed to piece it together. I fed the paper to the candle flame just seconds before Shelton entered without knocking. "Elizabeth, Princess of Wales, requires your attention, Lady Mary," she said. "Her napkin is soiled." She stepped to the rough table and picked up the charred remains of the message. "A letter from a lover, no doubt," she said, letting the black ash sift through her fingers. I rose to attend to Elizabeth. In a few months, she would no longer need napkins. With any luck, in much less time I would be free. I would be gone from England, from my father, and from all my enemies. Chapuys had written that the plan's details must remain secret. "In the meantime," he wrote, "resist the pressure to sign the oath, but do not put yourself in danger." Do not put yourself in danger. But I was in danger every moment of my life.

Chapter 18: A Desperate Plan

I remember leaving Hatfield before Christmas. Elizabeth's household was moved to Greenwich for the holiday celebrations. I remember our arrival and the news of Lady Susan's death. She had died in childbirth, and her baby boy had died with her. The loss of my cherished friend was a terrible blow. Within days, I fell ill. On New Year's Day, I lay in a palace chamber, tossing with fever.

Delirious, I begged to see my mother. Cromwell denied the request. Heedless of the danger, Bryan got word to Chapuys. He came at once and demanded to see me. He suspected poison and insisted the king allow my mother's physicians to examine me. Henry refused. He did not express deep concern, but he did send his own physician and the royal astrologer. They determined the sickness was caused by an imbalance of humors. They prescribed bloodletting and leeches. The fever gradually subsided, and the stomach pains lessened. But the illness and its treatment left me so weak I could barely walk.

Early in the new year, Chapuys visited me. "The king himself has requested I call upon the ailing Lady Mary," the ambassador announced loudly. He spoke to the women assigned by Cromwell to guard me. I was sure Chapuys bribed them to let him speak to me privately. "The plan is complete," he whispered when we were alone. "You must somehow give a sleeping draught to your guards. Once they are asleep, make your way out of the palace. Go through the garden to the boat landing." He continued, "Two boatmen will be waiting to row you to Gravesend. There, the emperor's ships are ready to sail with you to safety. But you must be prepared to leave on short notice. Once Emperor Charles sends his final approval, you will have only an hour or two. Will you be strong enough for this?"

"I am nearly strong enough now," I insisted. In truth, I could barely remain upright. "When can we expect Charles's approval?"

"There is no way of knowing. The emperor is in a difficult situation. By going against Henry, he risks upsetting the balance of power in Europe. I beg you to have patience and to trust me."

"The second part is easy," I replied. "I trust you with my life. The first part—patience—is far more difficult."

That night, I asked the physician for a sleeping potion. I told him I needed double doses to sleep. I hid the white powder in the enameled box from Reginald. Then I went over the plan again and again in my mind. I would ask my guards to join me in a cup of spiced wine before bed. This was a custom I would begin at once. On the appointed night, I would distract them while I slipped the powder into their cups. After they were asleep, I would dress in the rough countrywoman's clothes that Bryan would hide for me. In darkness, I would feel my way down the back staircase and into the garden. The gate would be locked but not guarded. I would climb a gnarled oak tree, crawl onto a limb, and drop to the ground. A boatman would be watching to help me if needed. I rehearsed the scene thoroughly in my mind. Now I had only to practice the patience Chapuys recommended.

Weeks passed with no word. I had recovered my strength. Then, soon after my nineteenth birthday, Bryan came to my chamber. "You are to leave," she said.

"Is it done then?" I asked excitedly. "Has the emperor sent his approval? When, Bryan, when?"

Bryan shook her head. "In three days' time. But you are not leaving for the Continent. You are to leave for Hunsdon Palace."

"Hunsdon? That is a day's ride from here! How will I reach the ship at Gravesend from there?"

"You will not. The king has grown wary. He suspects you will try to flee. He believes your mother and Chapuys are involved. He has ordered your removal to Hunsdon."

"Will my father not be satisfied until I am dead?" I cried, wringing my hands.

Bryan took me in her arms. "Hush, Mary, hush," she crooned, just as she had when I was a small child.

Banished to Hunsdon, I refused to give up hope. I continued to rehearse the escape in my mind. At least one thing had improved. Cromwell had decided I did not need guarding at such a remote place. Now I imagined myself walking in the countryside. Horsemen hired by Chapuys would swoop down and carry me away. It would be a pretended abduction. There would be a long, wild ride to Gravesend, where Charles's ship would wait. But when the secret letter finally came from Charles, it was not the message I wanted. "It is my intent," Charles had written, "to bring your father, the king, back to the True Church in Rome. Therefore, I ask for your patience, dear cousin. I beg that you do whatever King Henry requires of you."

I ripped the letter to pieces and stamped on them. Could my cousin be that slow-witted? King Henry required me to swear the double oath. Refusal meant a traitor's death. It was an impossible choice for me. Surely Charles understood that. Clearly, he did not care.

Late in the spring of 1535, I was ordered back to Hatfield. Once again, I served as Elizabeth's servant. Sometimes I adored her. Other times, I blamed my misery on her and wished she had never been born. That same spring, Parliament enacted new treason laws. They called for the death of anyone who spoke ill of the queen or criticized the king. Anyone suspected of treason had to be reported. Failure to do so was also a treasonous act.

The king's representatives gathered us together. One read out the penalty for treason as we listened in horrified silence. "Any person convicted of treason will be led back to prison. They will be laid on a hurdle and drawn to the place of execution. There the condemned is to be hanged and cut down alive. His private parts are to be cut off and thrown into a fire." The reading continued, "His bowels are to be taken from his living body and burned before his eyes. His head will be cut off, and his corpse paraded through the streets. His hands and feet will be nailed to the city gate. His head will be impaled on a pike on London Bridge, according to the king's will."

"He has gone mad," I whispered to Bryan. "Surely it's Anne who has driven him to this."

"Perhaps so," Bryan whispered back. "She is a desperate woman. My nephew told me rumors are flying. The king has tired of this queen and has taken a new mistress. Her name is Jane Seymour."

Jane Seymour? I remembered her. Lady Jane had been present during Anne's labor. I recalled her calm manner and simple kindness. Jane seemed the opposite of Anne. She was blond and pale with solemn gray eyes, quiet and refined. Anne was lively and often shrill. Jane was a gentle woman. But a match for the cruel man my father had become? It seemed laughable.

"There is other news," Bryan said. "The queen expects a child in the summer."

"Is it true? Or another of Anne's imaginings?"

"She has felt the baby move. A Te Deum has been sung in thanksgiving." News of a pregnancy was more important than rumors of a mistress. If Anne gave the king the son he demanded, her position would be secure. King Henry could have all the mistresses he wanted. Queen Anne would be invincible. But if she did not, then her time was finished.

Chapter 19: The King's Madness

Lady Margaret Bryan discovered the secret chamber at Hatfield. She told me all about it. "The room is hidden behind a false wall in the closet," Bryan confided. "It can be entered through the back of a tall linen cupboard. The other entrance is from the king's locked royal bedchamber." She continued, "Sir Francis has sent word that he will visit me soon. I will arrange for you to meet him secretly in the hidden chamber." Then she added, "I, of course, will be present to avoid any improper appearance."

I suppressed a smile. To whom would a secret meeting appear improper if no one knew of it? The real reason, I suspected, was that Bryan had always been fond of gossip. But her boldness surprised me. I never imagined the sweet-faced old woman had such courage. The secret chamber was cramped and airless. It was furnished with a damask-covered couch and silk pillows. It was simple for Bryan and me to slip into the chamber through the cupboard. But smuggling in a tall man was a challenge. Sir Francis had to wait in a smelly guards' toilet before Bryan signaled it was safe.

On a cold and stormy midwinter night, the three of us huddled in the dark. We were unwilling to risk lighting a candle. "Henry has begun to send representatives to the monasteries," Francis Peacham whispered. "He is demanding the monks swear the oath of supremacy. The monks all refuse. Henry is having them hauled off to the Tower to await execution."

"Has he truly gone mad then?" I breathed.

"I cannot say, madam, although many believe he is bewitched. He has enormous debts and is desperate. Once the monks are imprisoned, Cromwell seizes their lands. He also takes their silver chalices, golden candlesticks, and gem-studded crosses." I thought of Brother Anselm, my theology tutor, and other pious monks now in prison. But Bryan was hurrying us out of the secret room. "I have an ill feeling, like a cold hand upon my neck," Bryan murmured. "A feeling of evil all around us." So did I. We left our hiding place separately.

Ten days after New Year's, a hunchback in filthy rags appeared at Hatfield. Elizabeth was at Greenwich with the king and queen for Christmas. I had been left at Hatfield with only the servants for company. As I offered the hunchback a loaf of bread, he pressed a letter into my hand. It bore the seal of Catherine of Aragon. I hid it in my cloak and hurried to my bedchamber. It was the first letter from my mother in four years. My hands shook as I broke the seal. The handwriting was not my mother's.

"My dearest child," it began, "I am dictating these words to my good friend, Dr. Firth. I fear that by the time you receive this, I shall have closed my eyes for the last time. Your father ordered my removal to Kimbolton Castle. The place smells so of decay that my poor health has worsened. It is a frightening place. At night the wind howls, and doors slam on their own. I have kept to one chamber, leaving only for mass. Now I shall leave it once more, to go to my grave. I fear I am being poisoned slowly. Death is near." I put the letter down and prayed for strength to continue.

I have written to your father once more. I swore my everlasting love and pleaded with him to let me see you. I have kept alive by sheer will these past eight years since I last saw you. You were a lovely young girl then. Now you have grown to become a lovely woman. Nevertheless, your father remains firm that we are not to see each other. Tears poured down my cheeks so that I could scarcely go on. I wiped my eyes and read the final paragraph. "And so, I beg you, remain firm in your resolve. Sign nothing, agree to nothing. You shall be queen, as is your right and duty. I send you my love and my blessing." The letter was signed *Catherine, Queen*.

My mother's love had kept me alive through these wretched years. How could I continue without her? For a moment, I wanted to die, too, just to be with her. But I realized that for her sake, I must go on. My mother was right. By the time I received her letter, she was already gone. Cromwell himself came to inform me officially. My mother had died on the seventh of anuary. He confirmed I was not allowed to attend the funeral. "I beg your pardon for that, Lady Mary," Cromwell said in his lazy way. "But your father forbade it."

"Why?" I asked. Cromwell stared at me with his glassy toad's eyes. "Why am I not permitted to be at my mother's funeral?" I repeated.

"Reasons of state," Cromwell said. "The king wishes to avoid a popular display of support for you. It would not be in their best interest." His lip curled in a sardonic smile. "Nor in yours." He then fumbled in his leather pouch. He drew out a gold chain from which hung a cross. It was the one my mother had brought from Spain as a young bride. "She left you this,"

Cromwell said, carelessly letting it drop. "The king has determined it belonged to your mother, not the crown." As soon as he left, I ran to my chamber and fastened the cross around my neck.

Several weeks later, Bryan brought me a letter from her nephew. "After Catherine's death," Sir Francis wrote, "the king ordered his courtiers to dress in yellow to celebrate. He danced through the Great Hall with Princess Elizabeth in his arms. Queen Anne was heard to exclaim, 'God be praised! Now you only have to get rid of Mistress Mary and our future is assured.'" For once I did not care. I was so numb with sorrow that I felt no fear. Around that time, another disturbing rumor reached me. The embalmer of Catherine's body had confessed to her physician. He said that when he opened the body, he found her heart to be black through and through. It was a sure sign of poison.

By all accounts, my father seemed gripped by madness. He was by turns joyful or sad, energetic or listless. There seemed no peaceful middle ground. In an effort to cheer the king, his friends arranged a tournament. Henry never missed a chance to show his skill with a sword and horse. He bested several knights before he was knocked from his saddle, senseless. Word of the king's injury sent the queen into early labor. The next day, Anne gave birth to a stillborn son.

Chapuys arrived at Hatfield late in April, soon after these events. When Shelton and Clere descended upon him, he waved them away. "Your power is gone," he informed them. "Over and done with." "The king is unpredictable," he told me when we were alone. "But one thing is clear: he is done with Lady Anne. Henry raved at the queen when the child was lost, blaming her for it all."

"Is it true the king has a new mistress?"

"So it seems. Anne found him with Lady Jane Seymour on his knee. She threw a most unqueenly tantrum. She yanked a necklace from Jane's neck and drew blood. There have been no sons with Anne. In his mind, this makes the marriage invalid. He now claims she seduced him into marriage by witchcraft. I believe he will soon rid himself of Anne and marry Jane."

"But how can he?" I asked. "Another divorce?"

Chapuys smiled. "Nothing so complicated," he said. "Henry has given the matter to Cromwell." My heart quickened. "Then I shall be restored as his legitimate heir!" I exclaimed. Chapuys quickly dampened my spirits. "No, madam. Henry will marry Jane. You will still be a bastard. And since you have not sworn the oaths, your position will not change. You are still in mortal danger, Mary." Chapuys added, "The king is in a vengeful mood. He ordered the beheading of the bishop of Rochester and Sir Thomas More."

"But More was his dearest friend!" I exclaimed.

"No matter. Henry will kill anyone who stands in his way. Something in the king has died. His goodness has given way to evil impulses. There is no compassion to temper his cruelty."

"All of this is because of that woman," I said angrily. "Anne is a witch! She put a spell on him. Once he is rid of her, perhaps he can regain his soul."

"I, too, would wish it, madam," said Chapuys. "But my sole concern now is for you. Your position becomes more perilous with each day you refuse to sign. I do not want to believe your father will allow you to suffer the same fate as others. But neither can I guarantee your safety." After Chapuys had gone, I sat slumped at my table. Even if Anne was losing power, I was no better off. I was still alone. My hope of wearing the crown was more remote than ever. And I knew that if I did not relent, I would remain cast out—if I lived to tell of it. To sign was to go against everything I believed. I would show weakness where others had shown courage and died as martyrs. Not to sign was almost certainly to die. And as wretched as my life was, I still wanted to live.

Chapter 20: The Fall of the Falcon Queen

Scarcely a week had passed when Bryan burst into my chamber. Her gray hair was flying wildly about her wrinkled face. "My nephew has been arrested, madam!" she cried, waving a crumpled bit of parchment. "Francis, accused of adultery with the queen and thrown into the Tower! And Queen Anne herself taken as well!" She pressed the parchment into my hands and sank to the floor.

"Anne is in the Tower?" I began. But I stopped and read the scribbled message. Sir Francis had written only a few lines. He explained that he and four others had been charged with treason. The queen, too, was a prisoner. Bryan paced the floor in a hysterical state. I knelt and tried to console her. I was about to say that surely Sir Francis was not Anne's lover. We both knew how much he despised the queen! But I also knew that what Francis had done mattered not at all. The king had decided to get rid of them both. I rejoiced at my enemy's fall. But I was dismayed she had taken Sir Francis down with her. "We must not lose hope that Francis's life may be spared," I told the weeping Bryan. Privately, I held no hope for him or the others.

For days we prayed for God's mercy and waited for news. Poor Bryan could only weep and ramble. She blamed her misfortune on Cromwell. "Cromwell has concocted this tale," she wailed. "He invented the charges against Francis to convict the queen of treason." I thought she was probably right. At last, I received a long letter from Chapuys. He must have been confident that Shelton and Clere no longer dared interfere.

Chapuys wrote: "On the first of May, at a May Day joust, Queen Anne dropped a handkerchief near Francis Peacham. The king, believing this a signal to her lover, left the tournament. He called for Peacham, Norris, and Brereton to ride back with him. The next day, Henry ordered the arrest of all three men. A court musician named Mark Smeaton was also arrested. The fifth and most shocking was Anne's own brother, George. All were accused of adultery with the queen." "Anne was seized by Cromwell's men. They took her to the Tower by barge in broad daylight for all to see. She was charged with adultery, incest, and treason. The five men were charged with treason. All denied the charges. Then, under torture, Smeaton broke down and confessed."

I remembered Mark Smeaton. His musical talents had won him a place at court. I, too, had enjoyed his lively playing and sweet voice. Could he have been Anne's lover? I continued reading. "Smeaton's signed confession stated he had been hidden in the queen's chamber several times. He hid in a cupboard where sweets were kept. When Anne called for sweets, it was the signal for Smeaton to come out." "Next to confess was Francis Peacham. He admitted his flute recitals for the queen usually ended in lovemaking. Miraculous changes occur when a man is stretched upon the rack. Norris and Brereton also acknowledged their guilt. Only Anne's brother, George, steadfastly maintained his innocence."

The trial began on May tenth. The last to be tried was Anne's brother. He was damned by the testimony of his jealous wife. The viscountess swore Queen Anne had publicly stated the king was incapable of fathering children. Anne also said she had slept with several men. This was to ensure she would have a male child to pass off as the king's own son. "As I write this on May fifteenth," Chapuys continued, "Anne and all five of her 'lovers' have been found guilty. They are sentenced to death. Queen Anne is to be burned or beheaded, as the king pleases. They have but four days left to make their peace with God. Once this dreadful business is done, I shall call upon you." I was so upset I could not bring myself to show Bryan the letter. We resigned ourselves once again to wait and pray.

Three more days passed. Then Bryan, white as a ghost, wordlessly handed me a letter from Sir Francis. She leaned against the wall, moaning, while I read. "Dearest Aunt," he had written in a shaky hand, "take this as my farewell letter to you. I have not much longer to live. I swear to you my innocence, as I have sworn before the judges. But I have been put upon the rack and forced to confess. I am condemned to die, and I shall go to my fate as bravely as I can." It was dated the eighteenth of May. This was the twentieth. I said a silent prayer for Francis Peacham and went to put my arms around his grieving aunt.

True to his word, Chapuys arrived at Hatfield within the week. I greeted him immediately. "Is Anne dead?" "She is, madam. And the others also." I was nearly overcome by a mix of emotions. I felt elation that the false queen was gone. I felt compassion for stricken Bryan. And I felt sorrow for Sir Francis, who had taken many risks for me. The ambassador guided me to a seat in my favorite corner of the Hatfield Scent Garden. Amid the chamomile and violas, he described the events.

"It all began in April," he said. "Cromwell, on the king's orders, compiled a list of men rumored to be Anne's lovers. It may be that Cromwell himself invented the rumors. In any case, there was the incident of the dropped handkerchief." "Would she be so bold?" I wondered. "Anne was not stupid." "Exactly," he said. "But this all played into the king's hands. It solved his problem." "And were you present?" I asked. "I was. I was in the crowd as Anne was escorted from the courtroom back to the Tower. All looked to the ax heads of her guards for the verdict. Ax heads turned away from the prisoner meant innocence. The ax heads were turned toward the queen! People were afraid to utter a sound."

"But, my dear ambassador, why has the king chosen this way to rid himself of Anne?" "Because the king is in love once again. During the trials, King Henry courted Jane Seymour. He did, however, take time to divorce Anne before she died. This made Elizabeth a bastard. He visited Jane's barge every night, dressed in his grandest clothes. Drinking and dancing within sight of the Tower. I found myself disgusted at his behavior, madam." Disgusted, yes—so was I. But I was also relieved he was done with Anne, my worst enemy. And I was frightened. My father had clearly lost his reason. Even without Anne, I was still in danger.

"I have brought you a letter from Lady Kingston, wife of the Tower's constable," said the ambassador. "It describes Anne's final hours. Do you wish to be alone to read it?" "No, please stay," I begged. With trembling hands, I opened the letter and read. "She never thought she was going to die. Then came word that the king believed her guilty but would show mercy. She would not be burned for incest. She would be beheaded. As a further sign of compassion, Henry promised to send for the best swordsman from Calais. This was better than a clumsy axman. She had wild laughing fits. The next minute she would be on her knees sobbing. 'Who will save me?' One moment haughty, the next pitiable."

On May nineteenth, Queen Anne began her last day. Long before dawn, she was on her knees in prayer. Early in the morning, she called for her ladies to help her dress. Only two were willing to assist her. The rest had fled in fear. At last, she was dressed in a gray damask gown over a crimson petticoat. Over this, she wore an ermine-trimmed robe. Her long, dark hair was caught in a gold net. The letter did not mention if she wore her usual ribbon and jewel. Lady Kingston ended her letter with this: "I believe Queen Anne truly repented the wrongs she committed. It may surprise you to know that she prayed most strongly for your forgiveness, madam. She told me she knew now she had wronged you. She would go to her death more easily if she could believe you might pardon her."

The letter slipped from my fingers. Pardon Anne? I thought bitterly. Never. "Madam?" said Chapuys, who had been watching me. "Anne prayed for my forgiveness," I murmured. "Not unusual when one faces death," Chapuys said. "And much easier than when one expects to remain alive." "Were you there when she died?" I asked him. "I was. It was my duty as the Emperor's representative."

As the sun rose, the executions began. Anne was forced to watch as the five men were brought to the scaffold one by one. Blindfolded, each man knelt and placed his head on the wooden block. Each time, the executioner swung the heavy ax. The severed head rolled away, and blood spurted from the neck. Assistants quickly carted off the body. They gathered up the head to be placed on a pike on Traitors' Gate. First came Smeaton, broken by torture. Then Norris. Then Brereton. The fourth was Sir Francis Peacham. He met his fate bravely, with grace and humility. The last to die was George, Anne's brother. She was forced to witness them all.

"I prayed for Anne's death," I confessed to Chapuys, "but not for all this blood." "Indeed, there was a great deal of it," he said. "A new scaffolding had been erected on Tower Green for privacy. But so much blood flowed that there was not enough sawdust to soak it up. The axman called for servants to clean the mess. The small crowd was restless until Anne appeared. Then all fell silent." "And my father?" I asked. "Was he present?" "He was not seen. He may have watched from a window." "Did she speak?" I asked. "Not a word we could hear. She walked with her head held high, but she was trembling. Up each step, one by one. The executioner waited, his face concealed by a black hood. His great sword glinted in the sunlight. She removed her cloak and the golden net from her hair. She handed them to a maid, who ran away in tears. She knelt by the wooden block. It was scrubbed clean but still wet. She was offered a linen bandage and accepted it.

"We expected her to speak, to protest her innocence, but she did not. Her face was like white marble. She leaned forward and placed her head upon the block. Then she realized her long hair was in the way. With both hands, she swept it up over her head, exposing her white neck. We waited, scarcely breathing. I have witnessed many executions, but never one like this. The executioner raised his sword. It was as if the world stood still. Then the blade flashed downward. We heard the dreadful sound as it cut through bone and flesh. The head rolled from the body and was caught by an assistant. He lifted it by the black hair and showed it to the crowd. The black eyes seemed to stare. It was done. Queen Anne was dead."

Chapuys sighed. For some time, neither of us spoke. Suddenly the sweet scent of roses overcame me. I stood and began to walk back to the palace. "It is over then," I said finally. "My enemy is dead." Chapuys, matching his steps to mine, shook his head sadly. "Anne is dead, that is true. But you are far from safe. Your life remains in peril." Suddenly Chapuys bent forward and seized my cold hands. "You must sign the oaths, madam. Obey your father's wishes." "I obey only God's wishes!" I insisted, trying to pull my hands free. But Chapuys held on tightly. His dark eyes gazed into mine. "Listen to me, Mary. If you do not sign, Anne's fate will be yours. The king is a violent man. He has become more brutal than ever. It might sadden him to have you executed. It might even break his heart. But he will do it. It is his will against yours, and you cannot win." He released his tight grip. "I cannot bear to see you harmed," he said hoarsely. "I beg you, Mary—for God's sake, sign the oaths."

"Help me to escape from here!" I cried. "I would cross the Channel in a sieve if I could just leave England behind!" Chapuys shook his head sadly. "I would give my life to help you, madam. But I can do nothing. Forgive me." The ambassador bowed and left me at the palace door. After he had gone, I climbed to my chamber. I rested my head on my writing table and closed my eyes. I was utterly alone and surrounded by enemies. There was no way out. At that moment, my strength collapsed. My courage deserted me. I tried to pray but found no words.

Chapter 21: The Price of Peace

Cromwell himself brought the documents. He watched as I scrawled my signature, *Mary Tudor*. I left off the title I still believed was rightfully mine: Princess. I acknowledged King Henry VIII as the supreme head of the Church of England. I also acknowledged the rights of his legitimate children to inherit the throne. Most difficult of all, I acknowledged that I was an illegitimate child. My parents' marriage was declared incestuous. When I finished, Cromwell witnessed my signature with his own inky flourish.

Once the oaths were signed, guilt tormented me. I had betrayed my mother. I had failed to stand by my principles and suffer the outcome. Many others still refused to sign. The number of executions increased. Dozens of heads rotted on pikes at the Tower, a sickening sight. Many of the dead were monks whose monasteries had been seized. Others were simple, deeply religious country folk who believed the king was wrong. They had held out, but I had given in. They had remained strong while I had weakened and yielded. My torment grew at night, when I lay sleepless. During the day, headaches blurred my vision. I could not read or do my needlework.

Exhausted and in despair, I knelt in the palace chapel. I gazed up at the suffering Christ on the cross. "Have mercy on me, O God," I prayed. "Save me." In the gloomy silence, I thought I heard a whisper. It was as if the figure on the cross spoke to me. I peered up at the face of Jesus. My sight was too weak to see it clearly. Yet the voice was distinct. *You must live, Mary*, the voice said. *One day you shall be queen. You shall bring the church back to the True Church of Christ in Rome. Now go in peace.* I remember nothing more, for I fainted and fell to the floor.

Slowly, my life began to improve. Shelton and Clere were sent away. New nursemaids arrived to care for Elizabeth. I was able to enjoy her company without being her servant. I was given comfortable chambers again. I was free to come and go as I pleased. I was permitted ladies-in-waiting and servants as needed. Cromwell sent me a gift: a frisky little black mare. I rode it in the countryside nearly every day. My headaches lessened. I slept for at least a few hours each night. But I could not forget the heavy price I had paid.

King Henry had taken a new wife: Jane Seymour. "They were betrothed the day after Anne's beheading," Chapuys reported. "They wed ten days later. The king and his bride both dressed in dazzling white. Henry is investing a great deal of hope in this new marriage." At summer's end, I received word that King Henry and Queen Jane were coming to Hatfield.

They arrived with all the usual pageantry on a late August morning in 1536. Everything had been prepared for their stay. But I was not prepared for the sight of the enormous fat man. He limped slowly across the courtyard. In my mind, I still saw my father as I remembered him from my childhood. He was tall, strong, and boldly handsome. But that memory was nearly fifteen years old. This King Henry looked much older than his forty-five years. He no longer strode boldly but leaned heavily on a golden cane. It was rumored he suffered from a painful, unhealing sore on his thigh.

At Henry's side hovered his new wife, Queen Jane. She was pale-skinned and fair-haired, her mouth pursed primly. I was so nervous that I could barely stop trembling. Later that day, I was summoned to the king's chambers. A page announced me: "Your Majesties, presenting Lady Mary." I dropped to both knees. I rose and approached my father, kneeling a second and third time. Each time I bowed deeply.

"My precious Mary," said the king. "Arise." I obeyed. The king remained seated. I looked directly into his eyes. They were bloodshot and watery, sunk into mounds of fat. Purple veins marbled his swollen nose. His red-gold hair had faded to a drab, gray-streaked brown. Then he smiled; several of his teeth were missing. I could scarcely hide my revulsion at what he had become. It seemed all his cruelty was revealed in his face. Surely Anne had caused this change. She had poisoned his soul. He held out his hand to me. Still trembling, I bent to kiss it.

Then I turned to Queen Jane. She smiled at me most sweetly. "Mary," Jane murmured, reaching out with fluttering fingers. *Perhaps this woman will heal him*, I thought, forcing a smile. *Perhaps she can undo Anne's witchcraft.* But I did not truly believe it was possible. It was too late.

The king and queen stayed at Hatfield for several days. They taxed the cooks to provide food and drink for their large group. To my surprise, the king never asked about Elizabeth. She was just days away from her third birthday. Surely he knew Elizabeth had been partly in my care. But it was as though the little girl did not exist. She reminded him of Anne Boleyn.

Elizabeth had also been declared a bastard. Now neither of us could inherit the throne. We had been equally rejected.

The evening before they left, Queen Jane gave me a diamond ring. It was a token of friendship. The king gave me a thousand crowns to refresh my wardrobe. It was hardly enough, given the ragged state of my clothes. "We shall enjoy your presence at court this Christmas," Jane told me.

"Time to find you a suitable husband, Mary," my father boomed. "You are how old now?"

"Twenty, Your Majesty," I replied with a graceful curtsy.

"High time! High time!" the king chortled in a high, childish voice. He attempted a little hopping dance that ended in a groan. His face transformed again. "Would you like a man in your bed, little daughter?" he asked with a leer. "You would, do not deny it! And you shall have him!" The king feigned deep thought. "Aha! I have the perfect husband for you! We shall launch the plans immediately!"

"Who is it, Your Majesty?" I asked, barely above a whisper. Stunned by his behavior, I glanced at Jane. She seemed to be paying little attention to her husband's insane rantings.

"Cromwell!" he cackled. "My vicar general thinks well of you. He sent you a little horse, as I recall. What say you, daughter? I think it a perfect match!" I longed to say, "I would prefer death." Instead, I replied, "It is as the king wishes."

To my great relief, nothing more was said about marrying Cromwell. Other possible husbands were proposed, but none suited the king. Nor did they find me suitable. I was, after all, a bastard. And King Henry refused to offer a dowry large enough to make up for my lack of a title. At twenty, my life felt empty and useless. I had neither husband nor child nor crown. I was a prisoner of the king's madness. But I clung to the memory of the voice in the chapel. One day I would reign as queen of England and restore the True Church. That would be my mission.

Chapuys came one last time to say goodbye. The ambassador was returning to the Continent for a visit and a rest. He promised to return within the year. We walked together in the Knot Garden. Little Elizabeth was with us. Pretty as a picture, she dashed along the path ahead. She snatched flowers and poked them into her red-gold hair. She ran back to us, laughing.

"I am the queen!" she crowed, striking a pose. "Look at me! I am the queen!"

Chapuys and I looked at her and then at each other. "Mark my words," Chapuys whispered. "Your new enemy has declared herself."

I stared at him, shocked by his words. "She is only a child!"

"The child of Anne Boleyn," he said.

I thought he was wrong. The child was so charming. I held out my arms, and she ran into them. But years later, I would remember that day. I would understand the truth and wisdom of his words. My sister would become my nightmare, my enemy.

Printed in Dunstable, United Kingdom